"Tonight, I won't take no for an answer."

"I'm not your type," Georgina replied coolly.

Clayton's eyebrows shot up. Then after a moment a malicious grin sharpened his features. "Ah, yes," he said. "I'd forgotten. You're not a service provided by the hotel."

Georgina stared at him, determined not to betray her confusion.

"Don't worry, Georgina," Clayton continued. "I was inviting you out to dinner, not into my bed!"

Kay Gregory grew up in England but moved
to Canada as a teenager, and now lives with
her husband in Vancouver. They have two sons
who have recently moved away, along with two
ferrets, leaving them sole custodians of the family
dog! Kay has had more jobs than she can possibly
remember, the best of which is writing Harlequin
romance novels.

Books by Kay Gregory

HARLEQUIN ROMANCE

3206—BREAKING THE ICE
3243—AFTER THE ROSES
3270—GOODBYE DELANEY
3330—AN IMPOSSIBLE KIND OF MAN

ROSES IN THE NIGHT
Kay Gregory

Harlequin Books

TORONTO • NEW YORK • LONDON
AMSTERDAM • PARIS • SYDNEY • HAMBURG
STOCKHOLM • ATHENS • TOKYO • MILAN
MADRID • WARSAW • BUDAPEST • AUCKLAND

With thanks and appreciation to:

Jo Slade, Richard Kaczor,
Mary Horton and Lise MacDonald

Without whose knowledge of hotel housekeeping,
hotel kitchens, racing pigeons and apple-pie allergies,
I would never have completed this book.

ISBN 0-373-03358-3

ROSES IN THE NIGHT

CHAPTER ONE

THE phone rang six times before Room 23 picked it up. There was a pause, and then a growly male voice said, 'Yup. What is it?'

'This is Housekeeping, sir,' explained Georgina brightly. 'We were wondering if you'd like us to make up your room.'

There was another pause, longer this time, before the voice said, 'Can't you read?'

Georgina rolled her eyes at Jenny, who was hovering by the office door. 'Yes, sir, I can,' she replied, taking care not to sound defensive.

'In that case, may I ask what the devil you mean by phoning? Oddly enough, I put the "Do Not Disturb" sign on my door because I didn't want to be disturbed. That does not mean it's OK to disturb me by phone.'

'I'm sorry, sir. We thought you might want clean towels.'

'What I wanted,' said the voice, 'was to be left in peace to catch up on my sleep. However, since that is apparently beyond your comprehension, and I am now thoroughly awake, yes, I suppose you may as well supply me with your damn towels.'

'Of course, sir. I'll be right up.' Georgina hung up the phone and wiped the back of her hand across her forehead. 'Ouch,' she said to Jenny. 'Room 23 is *not* happy. I think I'd better take his towels up myself. He'd most likely eat you alive.'

'Oh, dear,' said Jenny, her big brown eyes wide with worry. 'I didn't mean——'

'Not your fault,' Georgina told her briskly. 'I was the one who made the decision to phone.'

Yes, and it wasn't one of your better decisions either, Georgina Kettrick, she told herself as she hurried up the wide, red-carpeted stairs.

'Do Not Disturb' signs routinely put Housekeeping in a no-win situation. If the day was over and the staff just about to go home, they had three choices: ignore the sign and knock on the door, phone the occupant from the office, or leave the room untouched. As the Willow Inn's official head of Housekeeping, Georgina had the final say. But if she chose wrongly it was not uncommon for guests to become rude, or even abusive. As in this case, she thought wryly. She'd called the wrong shot for sure.

She took a deep breath, parked Jenny's cart against the wall, and rapped sharply on the door of Room 23.

At first there was no response, and Georgina had just lifted her hand to knock again when the door was flung open by a naked man.

She closed her eyes.

'What the hell's the matter with you?' demanded the irate voice she'd heard on the phone.

Very cautiously, she raised her eyelids. And swallowed. After all, the man wasn't *quite* naked. But he might as well be, she thought dazedly. That brief white towel slung precariously around his hips covered only the bare essentials. And bare was the right word, she thought, forcing herself to hold her ground instead of following her immediate instinct, which was to turn tail and run for the stairs.

'Well?'

She jumped. The voice was no less irate than before, but Room 23 wasn't likely to simmer down if she continued to stand in the hallway clutching his clean towels to her chest like a shield.

'Nothing's the matter, sir. Here are your towels. And I'm very sorry we woke you, but Jenny—she's your maid—tells me the "Do Not Disturb" sign has been on your door all day.'

'It has. Because my flight was delayed and I was up all night. That, my dear girl, is why I was asleep. And if Jenny is my maid, why are *you* here?'

Georgina, who would be thirty next month, discovered that she didn't much appreciate being called this objectionable man's 'dear girl'. Although now that she was over her initial shock she had to admit that he was presentable as well as objectionable. That very visible body was in superb condition, and the dark eyes glowering down at her were deep-set and unusually compelling. Not the sort of eyes one looked away from...

Hold it, Georgina. She pulled herself up short. She would *not* be intimidated by this pirate of a man with the tousled black hair and wicked lips just because he had a pair of bedroom eyes.

'I came instead of Jenny because I didn't want her upset,' she told him evenly. 'You sounded very bad-tempered.'

'I am very bad-tempered.' His dark gaze flicked over her in a contemplative way that made her feel as she imagined a turkey must feel the week before Christmas. 'So why are you the sacrificial lamb?'

'It's my job. Here are your towels, sir.' Georgina handed them to him with outwardly unruffled composure. She was thoroughly ruffled inside, but she was determined not to let him know it.

'Your job?' He raised heavily winged, dark eyebrows. 'How interesting. I wasn't aware that Willow Inns provided that sort of service.' His gaze raked over her again, taking in her thin but well-proportioned figure. 'Yes, I believe I could be compensated for the unnecessary interruption of my sleep.'

Georgina backed hastily away. 'Willow Inns *don't* provide that sort of service,' she told him. 'I meant I'm the head housekeeper here. It's my job to deal with problems when they arise.'

'Ah. So I'm a problem, am I?'

He looked so menacing with his firm jaw thrust out aggressively, and his deep eyes glaring, that Georgina took another step backwards. Oh, yes, he was a problem all right.

'I hope not, sir,' she replied frigidly. 'Is there anything else I can get you?' When a slow, meaningful smile began to spread across his rugged features, she added a firm, 'I meant anything the hotel provides.'

'Hmm. In that case how about making my bed?' The smile became more pronounced, tinged with malice.

Help, thought Georgina. What do I do now? Go and fetch reinforcements in the shape of Jenny, thereby making myself look like a coward, which is probably exactly what he wants—or go into this horrible man's bedroom and risk a lot worse than loss of face?

Time for another judgement call. She'd been wrong about the phone call. She couldn't afford to be wrong now.

He was lounging against the door-frame with one hand propped above his head, looking wide awake and very sexy. Deliberately so, she was sure. But there was something about his stance, and the way he was looking at her, that convinced her he wasn't as dangerous as he made out.

Besides, he *had* been disturbed, he was entitled to have his bed made, and it was up to her to cope with the situation. She made up her mind to risk it.

'Of course, sir,' she said calmly. 'Excuse me.' Lifting her chin, she marched towards the door.

He didn't move, and she was obliged to duck under his arm. When her thigh brushed against the concealing white towel, she held her breath. But it stayed in place, and as she crossed the room she thought she heard the man behind her give a soft, satisfied chuckle. Then the door was closed with a click.

Georgina started to make the bed, determined not to betray that she was nervous. But when his towel came flying past her ears to land on an antique velvet chair beneath the window she let out an involuntary gasp.

The chuckle came again. Without looking up, she carried on with her task. He was moving about the room. She heard the cupboard door open, then the sound of water running. Doggedly she tucked in a sheet, and went on tucking and straightening until the tap was turned off and all sound of movement had ceased. Then the job was done, and she had no choice but to face him.

Cautiously she lifted her head. He was leaning against the wall with his hands in the pockets of jeans of the hip-hugging variety. His belt was unbuckled, and he was watching her with a small hard smile on the lips that she had earlier labelled wicked. As she looked at them now, it occurred to her that in other circumstances she might find them very seductive. In fact he was a remarkably attractive man in an unorthodox, tough sort of way. Except that she didn't find bad temper or bad manners at all enticing.

'Will that be all, sir?' she asked, keeping her features studiously blank.

'It's all I'm likely to get, isn't it?' he replied equably.

'No, sir,' said Georgina, deliberately misunderstanding him. 'If you'd like me to clean the bathroom——'

'Sure,' he said. 'Go ahead.'

She went ahead, and when she emerged again a few minutes later the room's impossible occupant was lying back on the bed with his ankles crossed and his hands loosely linked behind his head.

'Good afternoon, sir,' said Georgina firmly, when she saw that he was watching her with a confident speculation that, to her disgust, she found curiously exciting.

'Good afternoon. And thank you for waking me up,' he said cryptically.

Georgina hurried across the room and out of the door. Now what did he mean by *that*? she wondered, leaning against the wall to catch her breath, and congratulating herself on keeping her cool throughout the whole ridiculous episode. He'd been smiling that odd little smile again too, and it was exactly the sort of smile she didn't trust. She'd been housekeeper at Snowlake's Willow Inn for five months now, and it hadn't taken her long to learn to spot trouble when it came on two legs.

Without being in the least conceited, Georgina was quite well aware that men generally found her attractive. She was no raving beauty, but her short blonde curls, grey eyes and pert little nose, combined with a smile which she had often been told was too friendly, added up to a package that a lot of men, quite mistakenly, assumed was open to offers.

It wasn't that she didn't *like* men, thought Georgina, as she stowed the cart in a small room at the end of the oak-panelled hallway. It was just that she took her job seriously, and getting involved with salesmen or guests wasn't her idea of responsible professional behaviour. Nor was it likely to impress Mr Novak, who was hard enough to impress as it was.

She sighed, and stared glumly at a pile of frayed towels. Mr Novak was a major fly in the ointment of what would otherwise have been an ideal job. It was too bad that, of all the Willow Inns the new manager could have been sent to, Clayton O'Neill had chosen to send him to this one. But O'Neill, who owned the chain of exclusive Tudor-style hotels that dotted the West Coast of the US and Canada, made all the major personnel decisions. It was the absent owner who had inflicted Steve Novak on the Snowlake, Washington Willow Inn.

Georgina had been hired by the retiring manager, a soft-spoken, silver-haired gentleman, and for the first few weeks everything had run smoothly. Then the new broom had arrived to tighten budgets, make his presence felt, and do everything possible to upset the dedicated and enthusiastic staff. Except for Chef Alexander. Nobody upset Alexander. Not if they valued their jobs. But recently, thanks to Steve Novak's slave-driving interference, Georgina had lost two maids and a laundry assistant. She wasn't about to lose anyone else—which was why she had taken on Room 23 herself instead of delegating him to shy little Jenny.

Room 23. Georgina groaned quietly.

She loved her job, and she loved Snowlake. The peaceful lakeside town where for a while she and Gordon had been happy was the only permanent home she'd ever known. She had been so glad to come back that she would have taken any job that was offered. But this post at the Willow Inn had almost been a dream come true, especially as it tied right in with her training.

Room 23, on the other hand, was no dream. He was one of the pitfalls of her kind of work, and she thought it quite likely that he would complain to the manager. She shut the storeroom door with a sigh. If he was only staying for a night, it might not make a whole lot of difference. If not, there was a good chance he'd be an ongoing problem. And there was only one way to find out about that.

Georgina ran down the stairs to her office and grabbed the phone.

'Room 23?' said Lori from Reception. 'Just a second, Georgi, I'll check.' Georgina heard the sound of a keyboard clicking, and then Lori was back on the line. 'Mr Smith's reservation is open-ended, but he expects to stay a few more days.'

'Thanks,' said Georgina, hanging up.

So Room 23, alias Mr Smith, was not only ongoing, but unpredictable. Just her luck. Nor was it fair to inflict him on any of the less experienced maids. Which meant that either she or Agnes would have to cope. Agnes. A slow grin spread across her face. Agnes was efficient, outspoken and enormous. It would take the obnoxious Mr Smith quite a while to rake his bedroom eyes over the bulk of that redoubtable mother-of-eight's figure.

'Mrs Kettrick, I'm afraid I can't talk to you now.' Mr Novak, black moustache bristling, looked up from his executive desk with an impatient frown.

Georgina ignored him, marched up the long strip of red carpet he'd installed to give visitors the impression that they were approaching a throne, and dumped a pile of towels down on his blotter. 'Those purchase orders,' she said flatly. 'Have you signed them?'

'Purchase orders?'

'The ones for the towels. I can't go on putting garbage like this in the rooms.' She slapped a contemptuous hand at the frayed white stack on the desk. 'It makes us look like a third-rate motel. These are so thin they'll fall apart the next time we wash them.'

Steve Novak swallowed, the Adam's apple swelling in his throat. 'Mrs Kettrick, another time, please——'

Georgina began to see red. She'd been in an uneasy mood since her encounter with Room 23 the day before, and she wasn't used to fluctuating moods. Usually she had no problem holding her temper because she didn't have a great deal of temper to lose. But this morning the sight of two shelves of frayed and tired-looking towels had suddenly become a major irritation. She'd put the orders in weeks ago, but Mr Novak had refused to sign them because he said his budget wouldn't stand the expense.

'Mr Novak,' she said, her voice rising uncharacteristically, 'these towels are a disgrace to the hotel. I need those orders signed *now*.'

Mr Novak blinked and straightened his tie. For the first time since she'd confronted him, Georgina realised he was nervous. Strange. Her opinions had never fazed him before. In fact he'd ignored them.

'Mrs Kettrick, please. I'm busy. This is a bad time——'

'It's always a bad time for Housekeeping,' said Georgina, losing all sense of caution. 'But there's never any problem signing Harvey's orders for the bar.'

'The Tudor Bar happens to be our biggest money-maker,' said Mr Novak in a strangled voice. 'And I really can't discuss the matter now.'

She saw his eyes slant sideways, as if he'd seen a mouse in the corner. Following their direction, her gaze was riveted by a pair of elegantly crossed, trousered legs. The top one was swinging gently back and forth. Above it, strong, businesslike fingers were tapping pensively on the black arm of one of Mr Novak's leather chairs.

Georgina gasped. Audibly. That corner of the room was in shadow, because Mr Novak liked to keep his lamp full on the face of any intrepid member of the staff who ventured into his office. But now that she was looking in the right place she had no trouble making out the figure of a man. A man who had rather more clothes on than the last time she had set eyes on him, but was none the less recognisable for that. None the less attractive either, she noted reluctantly. No wonder Mr Novak had wanted her out of his office. Room 23 had been supplying him with ammunition. In other words, an excuse to replace Georgina Kettrick with a meek and mild yes-woman with no visible opinions of her own.

'I see you have company,' she said, deciding she had nothing to lose. 'So if you'll just sign the orders I'll be going.'

Mr Novak's face turned a mottled sort of orange. 'You, Mrs Kettrick, will most certainly be going,' he informed her, his voice cracking. 'Permanently. As of now.'

Georgina stifled the sinking feeling in her stomach and drew herself up to her full height. She supposed she should have expected that. She had always known Mr Novak didn't like her, but as long as she did her job and kept out of his way as much as possible he hadn't found a reason to fire her. Now, of course, his ego had been

fatally bruised. She had confronted him in front of a
guest. His pride wouldn't allow him to let it pass. Besides, the opportunity was too good to miss.

Her pride wouldn't allow her to show she cared. 'Very
well,' she said coolly. And then, because she wasn't a
saint and couldn't resist it, 'By the way, Agnes is going
on holiday next week. You do have a replacement for
her, don't you?'

When she saw him gulp, Georgina knew her guess had
been right. He had intended to make Agnes temporary
housekeeper while he looked around for a permanent,
and suitably biddable replacement.

Ignoring the man in the corner, she smiled sweetly and
started to leave the room.

'Just a moment.'

Georgina stopped in her tracks. That voice, so irate
and caustic on the phone, spoke with such potent authority that it never crossed her mind to disregard it. Very
slowly, she swung around to face the man in the shadows.

'Perhaps, Mrs Kettrick,' he said quietly, 'you would
care to explain the problem.'

'But I...' Her voice trailed off, and she glanced
doubtfully at Mr Novak, who was swallowing hard. His
Adam's apple was even more pronounced, and he was
making cracking noises with his knuckles.

'It's all right,' said the man. 'Steve didn't realise I was
interested.'

'But——' began Georgina again.

'Steve, would you please explain matters to Mrs
Kettrick?' snapped Room 23 impatiently. 'I think she's
about to tell me it's none of my business.'

As that was exactly what Georgina had been about to
tell him, she threw another doubtful glance at Mr Novak
and said nothing.

'Mrs Kettrick, this is Mr O'Neill. You may answer his question.' Mr Novak cracked another knuckle. His face was now more ivory than orange.

Georgina managed not to gasp. Was it possible——? Yes, of course it was. Room 23, alias Mr Smith, was not just a bad-tempered guest. He was Clayton O'Neill, the human dynamo who had worked his way up from desk clerk at one of the Hiltons to found his own chain of highly successful and very select inns—which were patronised by the rich and reclusive as well as by people who preferred restful, antique elegance to the chrome and glass anonymity of the average vast modern hotel.

She felt her temperature rising. Of all the devious, underhanded——

'I understood this gentleman was registered as Mr Smith,' she said coldly. 'Is there some mistake?'

'No mistake,' said Clayton O'Neill, standing up and moving into the light. 'I prefer not to advertise my visits in advance.'

'I see,' said Georgina. 'In other words you hope to catch your unwary employees painting their toenails, holding up the bar in the Tudor Room, or in compromising positions in the cloakroom.'

He smiled, a slow white smile that showed his teeth. 'No. As a matter of fact I hope to catch them doing their jobs. As for compromising positions, I find those usually occur in the bedrooms. Behind "Do Not Disturb" signs.'

The smile stretched, became even whiter, and Georgina found herself trying not to blush. Then it came to her that she didn't have to remain in this unnerving man's presence if she didn't choose to. She'd already been fired.

'Excuse me,' she said, turning away.

A warm, very masculine hand fell heavily on to her shoulder.

'Where do you think you're going, Mrs Kettrick?' asked the softly smooth voice of authority.

'Home,' said Georgina, starting uncomfortably at his touch. 'I've just been fired. Remember?'

'I didn't fire you,' he said quietly.

Georgina paused, turned back to stare up into eyes that were dark and obscurely amused—the sort of eyes that could draw you in and drown you if you let them . . .

She shook her head. 'Mr Novak fired me,' she told him. 'You were here.'

He took his hand from her shoulder and it fell against the dark cloth covering his thigh. 'I know. And this is my hotel. If I want you to stay, then you'll stay.'

Georgina frowned. What was he trying to say? That the job was still hers? Or was he just flexing the muscles of his power?

'What if I don't want to stay?' she asked.

'You have a contract,' he said coldly. 'Which you foolishly signed agreeing to give one month's notice of any intention to quit.'

He was right. In the heat of the moment, she had forgotten. 'You also have to give *me* a month's notice,' she reminded him.

'Or payment in lieu of. Which I don't choose to give, because I'm not planning to fire you at this time.'

'Then I quit.' The words came out before she had the sense to stop them.

He raised his eyebrows. 'Not for a month, you don't.'

She was still gaping at him when he took her upper arms, turned her around and said, 'Get on with your job, Mrs Kettrick. I'll talk to you later.' He gave her a little shove, and, feeling a bit like a child being told to clean her room, Georgina half expected him to add a quick pat on her rear.

But he paid her no further attention, and she walked quickly out of the office, too stunned to do anything but obey him. Besides, she needed time to think.

When she reached her own office, she collapsed into the chair behind her desk, which was practical rather than executive, and piled high with mail, catalogues and order forms, as well as assorted samples left by salesmen.

'Now what?' she muttered out loud, as the sinking feeling she had suppressed earlier began to move down to her toes. Obviously she still had a job. But she didn't feel like accepting favours from the great O'Neill. He was too confident of his power to make people do what he wanted. And once he'd gone back to his Los Angeles headquarters *she* would still be stuck with Mr Novak— who had never cared for her much because she wasn't good at bowing and scraping. He would resent her even more after this.

Georgina sighed. It was no good. Much as she loved her job, she would have to leave. But there was no way she was leaving Snowlake. This town where she had met and loved Gordon meant too much to her. It was here that she had discovered what it meant to belong, and for the first time in her life had put down roots. There were other hotels. With her qualifications she was bound to find some sort of job.

'What's the matter, Georgi? Had another run-in with Tom Snape?'

Georgina looked up to see Agnes looming in the doorway. Her eyes, which resembled currants stuck into dough, were bright with sympathy.

Georgina shook her head. 'No, it's worse than a pushy salesman this time, Agnes. It's Mr O'Neill. He's Room 23. The one I had the run-in with last night.'

'Oh, boy.' Agnes heaved a section of her vast thigh on to the edge of a stool that stood against the wall. 'What was he doing here?'

'Not was—is. He's still here. In Mr Novak's office. And I guess what he's doing is snooping.'

'Not snooping, Mrs Kettrick. It may have slipped your mind, but I happen to own this hotel. In the circumstances, I think I have a right to keep an eye on my staff.'

Georgina withdrew her gaze from Agnes's horrified face, and swung slowly round to stare at the door.

Clayton O'Neill stood in the opening, his lean body draped against the frame. His arms were crossed, his dark head was bent towards her, and from the retaliatory glitter in his eyes she had no doubt that she was in for serious trouble.

Usually she met trouble head-on. But when it came in the form of this virile, probably angry powerhouse, she had a feeling head-on might prove ineffective—not to mention unwise.

CHAPTER TWO

'I'M SORRY,' said Georgina stiffly. 'Of course you have every right to run your hotels as you please.'

'Thank you.' He made her a sarcastic little bow, then turned his attention to Agnes. 'Mrs Sawchuck, would you mind leaving us alone?'

Agnes lumbered off her stool, at the same time throwing a worried glance at Georgina, who, recognising that the older woman was concerned about the notorious O'Neill reputation, said quickly, 'It's all right, Agnes. Mr O'Neill and I have a few things we need to discuss. I'm sure he's not planning to seduce me.'

'Hmm.' Agnes threw an unabashed glance at her employer, who was grinning like a smug Cheshire cat. 'I guess he'd have his hands full if he tried it.'

'A charming prospect, Mrs Sawchuck.' His eyes gleamed with devilish humour. 'Unfortunately I don't have the time.'

Georgina gasped, and fought back an urge to slap his face, which she knew was unjustified in light of her own ill-advised reference to seduction. She was searching for a way to change the subject when Agnes, unfazed by the blatant innuendo, said calmly, 'Lucky for you, Mr O'Neill.' Then, apparently satisfied that her friend wasn't about to be assaulted at her desk, she stomped past him and shut the door with a snap.

'You didn't mind her talking back to you,' said Georgina, surprised that this self-centred man could take

Agnes's outspokenness with equanimity. 'And you knew her name.'

'Yes. Shouldn't I? She's worked for me for the past eight years. And I can't remember a time when she hasn't delighted me by speaking her mind.'

'I know, but——'

'But you've decided I'm a tyrant who expects the minions who work for him to function on automatic like nameless slaves, to be "snooped" upon occasionally by the big bad boss. Is that it?' He hitched a hip on the edge of her desk and leaned over her. His crossed arms were on a level with her chin, and he was so close that she could smell the faint, piney scent of his body. It was distractingly seductive and, unknowingly, Georgina moistened her lips.

Clayton O'Neill smiled unpleasantly. 'Well? Are you going to answer me?'

Georgina forced herself to concentrate on his question. 'I don't think you're a tyrant,' she said finally, 'although you have a reputation for expecting top performance from your employees.'

'And for getting it.'

'Yes. But nobody's ever said you're unfair.'

'You don't consider snooping unfair?' His full lips curled up in a way that made her feel like a very small mouse about to be demolished by a tiger. But she wasn't a mouse.

'Not if you do your own dirty work,' she admitted. 'You do have a right to know what's happening in your hotels. And I suppose if you announced your arrival ahead of time you'd find all the cracks had been papered over.'

'Exactly. Are you a crack, Mrs Kettrick?'

Georgina sat up very straight. 'I bet your pardon?' she said in her haughtiest voice.

'I said are you a crack?'

Not for the first time in this man's company, Georgina felt her temper rising. But instinctively she knew that was precisely what he intended. He was putting her to some sort of test.

'Not that I'm aware of,' she said tightly. 'I run my department as efficiently as I can given the circumstances—whether I expect to be inspected or not.'

'That's what I thought. What circumstances, Mrs Kettrick?' He leaned forward so that his face was just above her own.

Immediately she tried to push her chair back, but one of the casters was stuck, and it wouldn't budge. 'Just—circumstances,' she muttered.

'I asked *what* circumstances.'

Yes, she knew he had. And he was entitled to an answer. But the only honest one she could give him would come across as whining about Mr Novak—who was so anxious to impress the boss with his tight budgeting and high profit margin that he was letting the hotel go downhill.

'I guess,' she said reluctantly, 'that things would run more smoothly if——'

'If Steve Novak would let you purchase new towels?'

For the first time since this interview had started, Georgina saw that Clayton O'Neill was smiling with what appeared to be genuine amusement. The smile made him look younger, less forbidding, and infinitely more attractive—even though his mouth was still much too close for comfort.

'Yes,' she agreed, a little breathlessly, as her stomach lurched with inconvenient lust. 'That—that would help.'

'Mmm-hmm. Anything else you'd like?'

His eyes were velvet-black and gleaming. 'Like?' she muttered stupidly, wondering why her mouth had gone dry. 'You mean——'

'I mean is there anything Housekeeping can use that may save us from becoming a "third-rate motel"? That is what you called us, isn't it?'

'Oh. No, of course it isn't. At least...' Her thoughts scattered before she could put them into words. He really was far too close. Georgina gave her chair another shove, and this time the caster dislodged and she was sent spinning back across the hard plastic floor-protector to end up slammed against the wall.

'Ouch,' she gasped, as the impact shuddered up her spine. For a few seconds she just sat there, dazed. Then, as she struggled to stand, she felt firm hands grasp her wrists and draw her on to her feet.

'Are you all right?' he asked briskly.

She looked up, expecting to see dark mockery in his eyes. But they were suitably sober, and filled with surprising concern.

'Yes, I'm fine, thank you.' She wondered vaguely why he was still holding her, and why she liked the feel of his hands on her skin.

He smiled as if he guessed what she was thinking, let her go, and sat back on the desk. 'Good,' he said gravely. 'I prefer my staff with all their body parts intact.'

Georgina wasn't sure she trusted his reference to body parts, so she folded her hands and fixed her gaze on the wall.

'Mmm,' he murmured. 'You're suspiciously submissive all of a sudden, Mrs Kettrick. I'm not sure it suits you. Neither does that practical and proper black overall which makes you look like a Victorian housemaid.'

'I'm told that practical and proper black overall was *your* choice of uniform,' she informed him without changing her stance.

'I know. Very short-sighted of me.' He grinned. 'Why do you dislike me, Mrs Kettrick?'

'I don't.' She did, but she wasn't about to admit it. She suspected that he was the sort of man who would quite enjoy being disliked.

'Good. In that case I hope you don't still plan on leaving?'

'Of course I do. Mr Novak wouldn't want me to stay.' She straightened the belt on her uniform and smiled brightly at him as if she didn't mind.

'Mr Novak is no longer an issue. I just fired him.'

'You what?' Georgina swung round to face him. 'But you can't have. He has a wife and kids——'

'Along with severance pay. He should have thought of the wife and kids before ruining the reputation for excellence of one of my most popular hotels. I assure you it didn't take long for the rumours to reach me, Mrs Kettrick. It never does. That's why I'm here.'

'Oh,' said Georgina, relieved. 'I was afraid you might have fired him because of the towels.'

'And that would matter? What a soft-hearted creature you must be. I wouldn't have thought it.'

'Wouldn't you?' said Georgina, nettled. 'Well, it's no surprise to me that you're so ruthless.'

He shifted his thighs on the desk. 'Ruthless? Is that how you regard a healthy respect for sound business practice—which in the long run keeps people employed? I'd no idea you were so fond of Steve Novak.'

'I'm not,' she said, disliking the caustic note in his voice. 'But I suppose he was better than nothing.'

'I doubt it.'

Georgina eyed him doubtfully. He was perched on the corner of the desk now with his legs apart and his arms once more crossed on his chest. He looked tough and very sure of himself. She frowned, not understanding what he meant.

'But you must have a manager,' she insisted.

'Must I? All right, Mrs Kettrick, I'll find one.'

Georgina stared at the deep red of his tie as the germ of an idea began to form. When she sensed that he was about to change the subject, she said hurriedly, 'I could handle it.'

He raised his eyebrows in what she could only assume was derision. 'You? My dear Mrs Kettrick——'

'I have the qualifications,' she interrupted, resenting his patent incredulity.

'I've seen your qualifications.' She watched his black eyes harden in concentration, then flick over her as if he were sizing up a prize cut of meat. 'All right,' he said abruptly. 'As I don't have anyone immediately available, you'll have to do—until I find someone permanent. At least you know the difference between third-rate and first class.' He sighed. 'I suppose that's the best I can hope for.'

Georgina put a hand to her head. It seemed to be revolving in circles. On the one hand she was being offered, albeit grudgingly, the chance to manage this hotel that she loved. On the other, she was being told she was the best of a bad job and would only 'do' until someone permanent was hired.

Taking a deep breath, she conquered a foolish desire to tell him where he could put his wonderful job, and said calmly, 'I'll consider it on a temporary basis—provided you'll consider *me* on a permanent one.'

To her utter confusion, instead of giving her a straight answer, he cocked an eyebrow and drawled softly, 'Permanent in what sense, Mrs Kettrick?'

Georgina tried not to gnash her teeth. 'Surely you didn't think I was proposing to you?' she scoffed, injecting a wealth of disbelief into the words.

'It happens,' he said drily.

'Not this time. Sorry to disappoint you.' How conceited could this abominable man get?

'No disappointment, I promise. Merely relief. So perhaps you'd care to enlighten me.'

'Enlighten you?' She bit her lip, wishing she hadn't sounded like a parrot.

'About the kind of permanent basis you had in mind.'

Was he laughing at her? She could almost swear he was, though it didn't show. 'I meant,' she said icily, 'that I'll be happy to take on the management of this hotel provided that in three months' time you'll consider me for the permanent position.'

Georgina pressed her lips together as he looked her up and down exactly as he had done a minute before. But she had a feeling that this time he was weighing everything in the balance, including, quite possibly, her height, weight and measurements. She wished the thought didn't send a sizzle of excitement through her veins. The last thing she wanted was to feel any sort of attraction to this odious man.

'You're a woman,' he said finally.

'I thought I was. Does that make a difference?'

'It might.'

'I see. So are you telling me the mighty O'Neill is afraid of hiring a woman?' She put her hands on her hips and challenged him with her eyes.

'No, not afraid, Mrs Kettrick. Merely concerned that you won't be able to handle the job. I've just got rid of one incompetent manager.'

'I am not incompetent, Mr O'Neill.'

'I'll be the judge of that,' he said levelly. 'Very well, Mrs K, you're on. Three months, not one day more. At that time we'll discuss the matter again.' He glanced at his watch. 'Your day's almost over, isn't it? Go home and change into something pretty, and we'll seal the bargain over a meal.'

Georgina gaped at him. She had no desire to have dinner with this overbearing man. She wouldn't be able to eat anyway. And she certainly wasn't making herself pretty for his benefit.

An idea came to her. 'Are you inviting Mr Kettrick too?' she asked, smiling innocently.

'Nope,' said Clayton O'Neill. 'Don't play games with me, Georgina. There's no Mr Kettrick, and we both know it.'

He had called her Georgina. And, surprisingly, it sounded right. For a moment she had no other thought. Then she remembered what had prompted his comment.

'Of course there's a Mr Kettrick,' she said. 'His name's Gordon, and he still lives right here in Snowlake. I just don't happen to be married to him any more.' To her horror, she heard her voice begin to crack.

He smiled thinly. 'Which is why I have no intention of taking him to dinner. You amaze me sometimes, do you know that?'

'Why?' asked Georgina guardedly.

'Because I would expect a militantly modern woman like yourself to go back to her maiden name after getting divorced.'

'My maiden name is Darling,' said Georgina.

He brushed a hand hastily over his mouth. 'I see. All right, I won't make the obvious comment. Go home and get changed now, will you? I'll pick you up about seven.'

Georgina opened her mouth. Militantly modern she wasn't. But nor was she any man's doormat.

'Don't say it,' he advised, before she could get the words out.

'Say what?'

'That it's against your principles to fraternise with the wicked boss.'

She stared at him. 'How did you know?'

'It was written all over your face. So was the fact that you resent being told what to do on your own time. But as my manager, Mrs Kettrick, your time is mine from now on. My executive staff don't work regular hours.'

'No, just irregular ones,' muttered Georgina.

Surprisingly, he smiled. 'Is a business dinner with your employer so very irregular? If you could stop thinking of me as the Ogre of Room 23, I don't see why it has to be a problem. You might even enjoy it. Obviously we have a lot to discuss, and presumably we both have to eat. Or are you one of those boring women who exist on spinach salad and grapefruit?'

Georgina smiled back reluctantly. 'No,' she admitted. 'I like eating too much.'

'I'm relieved to hear it. That's settled, then.' He walked over to the door and held it open. 'Until seven, Mrs Kettrick. I have your address.'

Without quite knowing how it happened, Georgina found herself standing outside her office. Clayton O'Neill shut the door behind them with a decisive click, and strode off without waiting for her answer.

She brushed a lock of hair out of her eyes and stared blankly after his confident back. Definitely a power back, she thought. Mr O'Neill had a reputation for knowing what he wanted and going after it. Now she knew why. But the question was, did *she* intend to do what he wanted? Tapping her foot against the shiny grey tile of the floor, she came to the reluctant conclusion that she really didn't have a lot of choice. She wanted the job, *he* wanted her company over dinner, and he was entirely capable of withdrawing his offer if she didn't fall into step with his plans. As long as his plans didn't include bed—he had a reputation on that score too—she supposed she would have to put up with him.

With a sigh of exasperation Georgina headed out to the car park to start her car. So much for her peaceful evening at home.

As always, she felt a quiet thrill of pleasure when she pulled up outside her very own cottage. It was the home she had dreamed of all through the rootless years on the road with her parents when she had longed so much for stability—the home she and Gordon had never been able to afford. It wasn't right on the lake, of course, but she could glimpse the water through the trees at the bottom of her gently sloping lawn. And it actually had a white picket fence with a gate, and yellow roses climbing the white walls.

As she took her key from beneath a pot of geraniums beside the door, a soft sound made her glance at the sky. A dozen or so pigeons, their wings barely moving in the summer air, were returning to their loft next door. Georgina smiled. Gordon's beloved racing birds. Now she knew for sure that she was home.

She waved at the pigeons, and a scruffy teenager slouching along the road thought she was waving at him and stopped to stare. Shrugging, she put the key back beneath the flowerpot.

The moment she opened her door, the comfort of the cottage enfolded her like a warm, friendly cape, and for a few minutes, as she made herself tea and put away the breakfast dishes, she felt at peace.

It was a peace she knew wouldn't last. Mr O'Neill would undoubtedly see to that.

All the same, by ten to seven she was ready for him, wearing what she hoped was the executive look. Unfrivolous black, suited to a sober discussion of the care and running of a sedate and successful Willow Inn.

'Good grief,' said her employer, when he arrived at her door exactly on the stroke of seven. 'Mrs Kettrick, I said pretty, not prudish. Were you under the impression I meant to misbehave?'

Georgina fixed him with her best steely grey stare. 'No, I understood this a *business* dinner, Mr O'Neill.'

'Ah. And you never mix business with pleasure? Very well, Mrs K, but I never mix dinner with depression. Take it off.'

'I beg your pardon?' said Georgina, drawing herself up to her full five feet five and adopting the voice she used on importunate salesmen. 'I don't remember agreeing to provide you with an evening's sleazy entertainment. If that's what you had in mind, you can leave. I don't need your job that badly.'

She half expected to be treated to another demonstration of the O'Neill temper. But to her total confusion he threw his head back and let out a shout of laughter. 'Do you always jump to conclusions so quickly?' he demanded, lowering himself into a cream-coloured armchair with a pattern of dainty pink daisies. 'If you do, I think I may live to regret that job offer.'

Georgina pursed her lips and hoped she wasn't going to blush. 'I thought you meant——'

'That I expected a certain payment for your dinner. Yes, I know, and I find the suggestion surprisingly offensive. What I really had in mind for you, Mrs K, was a speedy—and solo—trip to your bedroom, to remove that black abomination and substitute something appropriate to the occasion. We're going to the Pelican, my dear girl, not a funeral.'

Georgina glanced down at her sedately pleated dress with the round white collar. It had served her well for interviews and the odd funeral, and she had thought it entirely appropriate for Mr O'Neill—discouraging, in case he needed discouraging, but businesslike. Still, he had a point. It really wouldn't do for midsummer at the Pelican, which was Snowlake's most exclusive dine-and-dance spot. She had thought they'd be going back to the Willow Inn.

'All right,' she said, feeling exceptionally foolish for having so quickly misjudged him. 'If you'll wait just a minute, I'll change.'

He nodded, and settled back in the chair, his eight-foot-long legs disarranging the pink and brown rug at his feet. 'Something scarlet, I hope,' he called after her as she hurried from the room.

Georgina shoved her one red dress to the very back of the cupboard and pulled out a blue flowered cotton. It had a full, gathered skirt, petal sleeves and a softly rounded neck. Demure without being dowdy, she decided. It would do very well for the Pelican, if not for Mr O'Neill's exotic tastes.

'Better,' he announced from the depths of his arm-chair as she slipped back into the living-room. His gaze ran over her in that way she was becoming used to. 'But hardly inspiring.'

'Good,' said Georgina. 'You can do without inspiration. That's one thing I hear you don't lack.'

'How kind of you to say so,' he replied, with a grimace that looked suspiciously like a grin. Then, after glancing round her small, comfortable room with its brick fireplace, rose-coloured curtains, bright chintz chairs and lovingly polished hardwood floor, he added casually, 'You've managed remarkably well on a head house-keeper's salary, Mrs K.'

Georgina looked at him suspiciously. 'Are you suggesting I'm making a bit on the side?'

'No. Could you do that?'

'Of course I could. Salespeople are always trying to pressure me into choosing their products for the Inn.'

'But you, of course, are much too highly principled to be pressured.'

'Yes, I am. I'm also too busy.'

He nodded. 'I'm inclined to believe you.'

'Well, thank you, sir.' She laid on the sarcasm with a trowel. When his only response was to lift his eyebrows slightly, she added, 'It's none of your business, but I inherited a small legacy from an aunt. I bought this house with it.'

'As you say, none of my business,' he agreed. 'If it had been, the pink curtains and daisies would have been out.'

'Oh,' said Georgina, surprised to find that his criticism hurt. 'You'd choose black leather and dead rugs, I suppose, with a lot of heads and whips on the walls.'

'Heads and whips?' His eyes gleamed at her as he slowly uncrossed his legs and stood up. 'No, fortunately my tastes don't run along those lines.'

'Scalps, then,' she amended, backing away as he advanced towards her looking purposeful. 'Female ones.'

He laughed. 'Oh, I've collected a few of those in my time, but I tend not to hang them on walls.'

'I'll bet,' said Georgina, who could imagine where those heads would be laid—on his pillow, with his deep eyes glinting down at them... She swallowed, took another step backwards. That image was altogether too evocative...

He laughed again, softly, and when she stood with her back against the pale cream wall and couldn't go any further he came up to her and placed one gloved hand on her cheek. 'Watch it, Mrs Kettrick,' he warned. 'I could become the Ogre at any moment.'

Georgina didn't doubt it. As he took her arm to steer her out to a waiting limousine, she was forced to admit that Clayton O'Neill was proving a very disturbing man to be around.

The Pelican was beginning to fill up by the time they got there, but they were shown at once to a corner table on a glassed-in balcony overlooking the snow-fed lake from which the town had taken its name. A bucket of champagne arrived almost before they sat down.

'To my new manager,' said Georgina's host, raising his glass. 'May our *business* association prosper.'

She heard the slight emphasis on the 'business' and nodded coolly. 'To the Snowlake Willow Inn,' she replied. 'May *it* prosper.'

'It had better,' he said, with just the hint of a threat in his voice.

Georgina hoped he didn't notice the sudden rise of goose-bumps on her arms. What if she had bitten off more than she could chew? This man would be utterly ruthless if she failed him. He'd proved that by his treatment of Steve Novak. With O'Neill there would be no second chances. Severance pay and abrupt dismissal would be her lot.

When she saw him watching her as if he knew just what she was thinking, she straightened her shoulders and smiled as if she hadn't a doubt in the world.

During most of the meal they did indeed discuss business. Her employer made clear exactly what he expected of her, which was total dedication to the job. Georgina had no problem with that. In the months since she had worked at his hotel, she had grown to love its quiet antique elegance and charm. Every time she stood at one of the bow windows overlooking the sweeping expanse of lawn above the lake, she had a sense that at last she had come home. She was proud of the Inn. When Mr Novak had started cutting corners, she had taken it personally, as if the place really were her own.

When the coffee came, her companion changed the subject abruptly.

'Your employment records show you've been away from Snowlake for some years,' he informed her. 'What brought you back?'

'I always meant to come back,' she said, surprised he should ask. 'I was married here——'

'Unsuccessfully,' he interrupted.

She lowered her eyes and started to talk much too quickly. 'Yes, but we were happy at first. We married too young. I was seventeen and Gordon was eighteen. We met when my parents came here to do a show. They were a comedy team, and——'

'Yes, I know. Slow down, Mrs Kettrick, you *are* permitted to take a breath.'

Georgina grinned sheepishly, and carried on at a more normal pace. 'They always took me with them when they could. Sometimes, in the middle of the school year, though, they let me stay with my aunt Helen. She never paid much attention to me, but she was kind in a vague sort of way. She's the one who left me the legacy.'

'That doesn't explain why you came back. Or why you went away in the first place for that matter.'

Georgina couldn't imagine why he cared. But perhaps he was just making conversation. 'I didn't want to go,' she explained. 'I came to love Snowlake in the two years we were married. I'd never had a permanent home before, and it was heaven. Then after Gordon told me—told me he didn't want to be married any more...' She paused, stole a quick glance at his ungiving face, and hurried on. 'After that I tried to support myself by cleaning houses—it was the only thing I knew how to do. I managed all right, but I knew that if I ever wanted to get anywhere sooner or later I'd have to take some sort of training. So when I'd saved enough money I went away to college, got myself a job as a waitress, took home economics and some courses in hotel administration——'

'I've told you I'm aware of your qualifications, Mrs Kettrick.'

'Georgina,' she said, surprising herself. 'Would you mind calling me Georgina? It's less—formal.'

'Well, well, well. And I thought you were so wedded to formality. OK, Georgina. Why don't we really let our hair down? You can call me Clayte.'

'Clayte?' She blinked, and wished she hadn't.

'It's what my friends call me. You are my friend, aren't you—Georgina?'

Oh, dear. She didn't trust that sensuous little half-smile on his mouth.

'Yes, of course,' she said quickly. 'Why—er—Clayte? Instead of Clay?'

The smile became more pronounced and showed his teeth. 'I've been told Clayte is more appropriate,' he said.

Yes, she supposed it was. There was nothing malleable or clay-like about this man. Any person who tried to mould him into shape was destined to fail.

'We're straying from the subject,' he pointed out. 'You were telling me that you took courses——'

'I did. And afterwards I took a job as assistant housekeeper at a big hotel in Sacramento.'

'I know that. Why?'

'It was offered to me, and I'd run out of money. Then Aunt Helen died——'

'And you came flying back to Snowlake like one of those damned pigeons I dodged on my way into your house.'

He sounded contemptuous. Georgina frowned. He had no right to despise her for returning to the town where for the first time she'd had a chance to make friends, to get to know ordinary people of her own age instead of the footloose and unconventional characters her mother and father tended to gather round them.

'Yes,' she answered him shortly.

'Hmm.' He stared at her for a moment. 'Couldn't your parents have helped you?'

'My parents?' She gazed at him blankly. 'My parents never had much money. They stay in Florida now, but I honestly don't know what they live on.'

Clayte stirred his coffee. 'Your childhood must have been remarkably unrestricted.'

Georgina stared at his firm fingers holding the spoon. There was something in his eyes she couldn't fathom. And he sounded quite unreasonably bitter.

'It was remarkably chaotic, totally insecure, and often lonely,' she informed him. 'I was glad to grow up. Is that what you mean by unrestricted?'

Clayte shrugged. 'It doesn't sound so bad. And I don't see why it turned you into such a paragon of small-town domesticity.'

Without meaning to, Georgina gasped out loud at the biting contempt in his voice. What had she said to deserve *that*? 'Is there something wrong with domesticity?' she asked tightly. 'My eye for domestic detail hasn't done your hotel any harm.'

'I suppose there's a place for it,' he agreed. When she didn't say anything, he added with a touch of impatience, 'I've offended you, haven't I?'

'Does it matter?'

'Not particularly. But I do prefer to keep my staff happy.'

'I'm perfectly happy, thank you. It's a matter of total indifference to me whether you approve of my domestic arrangements. And I happen to like pink curtains and daisies.'

'So did Shelagh,' he said grimly.

'Shelagh? Your wife?'

He smiled, the piratical smile that had so unnerved her from the first. 'Hardly. She and I were—you might say *friends*, for a number of months not long ago—until the day she decided to bake me an apple pie.'

'Surely that wasn't a crime.'

'Not a crime, no,' he replied bleakly. 'But I have learned, my dear Georgina, that apple pies and aprons are inevitably followed by instructions to wipe my feet, keep my fingers off the walls, tidy my room, and avoid spilling crumbs on the carpet. I perceived that Shelagh was about to become a very domestic bore—possibly one with incipient nesting instincts.'

'I see. You prefer the slinky, sophisticated type, do you? The kind who go in for diamonds and long-deceased mink.'

Clayte put his napkin on the table and fixed her with a malevolent black eye. 'I prefer the carefree, unattached type, Georgina. So don't even think of baking me a pie.' He stood up and held out his hand. 'Come on, let's see you slink. I have a feeling you'll do it rather nicely.'

Georgina grasped the edge of the table. 'What?' she gasped. 'What are you talking about, Mr——?'

'Clayte. Come and dance with me, Georgina. Haven't you noticed they're playing our tune?'

'We don't have a tune,' she said, swallowing.

'No, but we soon will have. Up you get.'

The band on the raised platform across the room was playing 'Some Enchanted Evening', but for the life of her Georgina couldn't see that there was likely to be anything enchanted about dancing with Clayte. Stimulating, yes, even erotic, but enchantment didn't go with this sensual, hard-headed man. Besides, she didn't want to dance with him. Instinct told her it would be a mistake.

'Georgina, don't force me to prise your fingers off the table, please. I asked you to dance, not sell your soul.'

Around them conversation began to die away, and she realised they were attracting attention. Clayte was the sort of man who would always attract attention, she supposed. And he didn't care if people were staring.

Very reluctantly, she allowed him to draw her on to her feet. When they reached the dance-floor, instead of placing a circumspect hand on her back, Clayte clamped a firm arm round her waist and pulled her to him. She could feel the steady beat of his heart and the hardness of his firm body through her dress.

The band, which tonight appeared fixated on old musicals, started to play 'We Could Have Danced All Night', and as the murmurous music and the heat of the summer night enveloped them in an age-old magic Clayte began to guide her smoothly around the softly lit floor.

For a few seconds Georgina forgot she was dancing with her boss, and gave herself up to the music and the moment. Then Clayte bent his head and whispered into her ear, 'I knew you'd slink beautifully, Georgina.'

Heat flooded her face, and she tore herself out of his arms and ran through the nearest exit into the night.

CHAPTER THREE

GEORGINA leaned against the wooden wall of the low building and put both hands to her head.

What had come over her in there? Why had she felt this overwhelming need to get away just because Clayte had made one teasing, half-suggestive remark? Clayte… Funny, it seemed natural to call him that now. But why had she run from him? She wasn't a giddy fifteen-year-old any longer, unable to handle a bit of careless banter.

She rested her head against the wall and listened to the lake whispering to the shore. At its edge, the shadowy fronds of willow trees stirred like giant feathers in the night. Gradually she began to feel safe again, secure on her own familiar ground. She hadn't needed to run from Clayte after all. He was no ogre. Just an extraordinarily compelling man who for some reason made her feel afraid. Yet he had done nothing explicit to frighten her. It made no sense.

'Georgina? What the hell are you doing?'

Georgina closed her eyes. She might have known he'd come after her.

'Just getting some air,' she lied quickly. 'I felt faint.'

Probably he considered fainting spells boringly unsophisticated and dull, but she couldn't help herself. No way was she telling him she'd been overcome by a fit of mindless panic of which he was the unwitting cause.

'Then why didn't you say so?' She could just make out his features as he emerged out of the shadows in front of her, and she saw his heavy brows come together. 'You're not——?'

'No,' said Georgina tiredly. 'I'm not pregnant. It takes two to tango.'

'So it does.' Not a muscle in his face was moving, and his voice was soft as smooth silk. 'I take it you don't tango, then, Georgina?'

'Not at the moment,' she said coolly, unwilling to let this overpowering man know that she had only had one serious romance since Gordon. And that hadn't lasted long either, because she had always been busy studying or working. Understandably, Ben had speedily got tired of waiting around—and when he left her she hadn't minded nearly as much as she expected. Sometimes she suspected that her brief marriage to Gordon had made her over-wary of love.

Clayte reached out to take her by the arm. 'Good,' he said. 'Can't have my new manager distracted from her duties. I'll take you home now, shall I? I don't want you getting sick on me either.'

'I'm not sick,' said Georgina. 'It was just the heat.'

'Mmm,' murmured Clayte non-committally, and she wasn't sure if he believed her or not.

When another limousine delivered them to her gate, he got out and escorted her to the door. Then, as she was fumbling for her key, he put a hand on her shoulder and turned her until she was facing him. She looked up, startled, and tried to shake him off. But he wouldn't release her, and his deep eyes studied her face in the moonlight as if he was trying to see into her mind.

'What's the matter?' she asked shakily. 'Have I got spinach on my teeth or something?'

'You didn't order spinach.'

'Didn't I? Oh. Well——'

'Don't worry. I'm just checking on the state of your health. Spinach or no spinach, I wasn't planning to kiss you. Kissing my managers isn't something I do. It's bad for morale.'

'Oh, is it?' said Georgina, getting back her wits and her breath at the same time. 'Well, I promise you it will be bad for *your* morale if you try it. *I* don't believe in kissing men who think they were put on earth as a special favour to women. Now, if you don't mind, I'd like to go in and get some sleep.'

Clayte nodded. 'I don't mind at all. A good night's sleep should do wonders for your disposition. Why don't you open the door?'

Georgina glared at him, which only made him smile, so she pushed her key into the lock and turned it. But before she could stop him his hand was on her back and he was pushing her gently inside.

'You can't...' she began, rounding on him.

He ignored her, put a finger beneath her chin and lifted her face to the light. To her horror, she felt an odd lassitude creep over her, a slow, enervating warmth that seemed to stem from the place where his hand was connecting with her skin.

'OK,' he said, after searching her features with a hard-eyed thoroughness which reminded her that he hadn't got where he was without learning how to make snap judgements. 'I think you'll do. You didn't feel faint at all, did you?'

'I did. I do.'

He dropped his hand abruptly. 'Is that so? Are you telling me you're subject to Victorian vapours? I'd never have thought it.'

Georgina was about to tell him that she was subject to twentieth-century aversions to discourteous men when he swung around, said, 'Goodnight, Georgina. I'll talk to you in the morning. Don't be late,' and disappeared into the darkness.

Georgina closed the door slowly behind him, sank down into her favourite armchair and passed a hand over her eyes.

What an extraordinary evening it had been. Oh, not the first part. That had been nice, once she'd given in to his lordship's taste in clothes. She didn't often get to ride in a limousine, the food had been excellent and the business part of the evening had been productive. Clayte knew what he expected of her, and she liked that. But somewhere along the line the conversation had turned personal, and from that point on she had felt as if she was standing on quicksand. Which wasn't a bad analogy, she supposed. Any woman who got too close to Clayte could very easily succumb to the powerfully seductive pull of his personality—not to mention his physical presence.

Georgina sat up and, although there was nobody watching, tugged her dress down to cover her knees. Luckily she needn't worry about his powers of seduction, she told herself. He wasn't interested in ordinary women who liked housekeeping, gardens and apple pies, and he disapproved of fraternising with his staff as much as she did. His concern for her welfare didn't extend beyond her ability to manage his hotel.

As for that episode on the dance-floor, he had asked her to dance because it was the social thing to do. And she had reacted like a nervous teenager because he was a hard, sexy hunk with a glorious body, and it had been a long time since she'd been anywhere close to a man. She didn't go out much because she couldn't afford it, and the men she met at the Inn mostly had one thing in mind...

With a small, half-formed sigh, Georgina stood up and wandered into her bedroom. One day, perhaps, she would meet someone who wanted the same things she did, someone she could love with all her heart. But if that day ever came she was sure he wouldn't be at all like Clayte O'Neill.

All the same, she fell asleep dreaming of danger—and wickedly smiling white teeth.

'Georgi, is it true? Are you really the new manager?'

Georgina paused as she hurried past the reception desk, where red-haired Lori was busy arranging post-cards. 'I think so,' she said, grinning. 'I still can't quite believe it myself.'

'Neither can I,' said a clipped voice from directly behind her. 'Mrs Kettrick, the air-conditioning in my room doesn't work. Why doesn't it?'

Georgina swung round. 'I don't know, it was fine yesterday. Housekeeping doesn't deal with——'

'You, Mrs Kettrick, are no longer Housekeeping. Agnes has agreed to change her holidays, so she will be in charge of that department until you find someone to take the job on a permanent basis—or until I demote you.'

She stared at Clayte's strong, determined face. He looked as if he'd been up and causing trouble for hours.

'I'll see to the problem,' she said crisply, walking past him with her chin in the air.

But when she reached her office she discovered that he was there ahead of her. 'Wrong office, Georgina,' he drawled. 'If you want to be one of my executives, you'll have to start thinking in terms broader than clean sheets and clean bathrooms.'

'Housekeeping involves considerably more than that,' she said tartly.

He leaned against the wall and folded his arms. 'That, my dear Georgina, is something you don't have to tell me. I'm an authority on the dreary art of housekeeping. However, my managers do not conduct my business surrounded by samples of shampoo and soap. Nor do they concern themselves with the whiteness of the wash.'

Georgina heard the note of raw contempt in his voice and wondered what acid was eating away at him now.

'You think I can't handle it, don't you?' she accused him.

'The possibility has crossed my mind, I'll admit. Three months, Georgina. In the meantime, you'd better move into your new office. And don't forget I want my air-conditioning fixed.'

'Yes, sir,' said Georgina woodenly. 'It will be. And I'll move my office later, if you don't mind. I have one or two more pressing matters to deal with.' She sat down behind her desk and began to press buttons on her phone.

'I do believe I've just been dismissed,' said Clayte softly. 'OK, Georgina, I'll await results.'

She ignored him, and when she looked up he'd left the room.

To her enormous relief, he stayed out of her way for the rest of the day, and she was able to get down to her new job unhindered by his incendiary presence. It wasn't easy explaining to the other department heads that she was now their boss, and when she called them all to a meeting she was half afraid that Clayte would materialise like Big Brother to embarrass her with his critical presence. But he didn't, and by the time the meeting was over she was fairly sure that Michael and Harvey, who ran the dining-room and the Tudor Bar respectively, were reasonably reconciled to her new status. Miss Duncan, who ran the office and had been Mr Novak's assistant, was not. And Chef Alexander was an unknown factor. He had always been a law unto himself, but Georgina felt that as long as she left him alone to do what he already did so well there was no need to anticipate trouble.

In that she was wrong, but the trouble didn't come from Alexander. It came from Miss Duncan.

'Georgina,' she called, her blue-rinsed head bobbing up and down as everyone else filed passively out of the boardroom. 'I'd like a word with you, please.'

Georgina paused. 'Yes, Miss Duncan?' Nobody ever called Miss Duncan by her first name, which, according to personnel records, was Gertrude.

'Do you really think you can fill Steve Novak's shoes?'

'No,' said Georgina, who'd had a very long day. 'At least size eleven, I'd say.'

Miss Duncan's trap-like mouth tightened. 'I hardly think it's a laughing matter, do you? The dear man has a family to look after. He's been good to me.'

'I'm sure he has,' Georgina nodded, knowing that her indignant accuser had been amply rewarded for telling tales on her fellow staff members. 'It wasn't my decision to fire him, you know, and I *am* sorry he's out of a job.' She smiled bracingly. 'If you and I are to work together, though, we'll have to forget about our personal feelings, won't we?'

Miss Duncan's eyes slanted evasively sideways. 'Yes, of course,' she agreed, in a cloyingly ingratiating tone. 'I'll do my best, Georgina.'

'I'm sure you will,' said Georgina, who wasn't sure of anything of the sort. She knew that if she had any sense she would fire the resentful assistant on the spot. But she couldn't do it. She wasn't used to dismissing people, and compassion won out over sense.

By five o'clock she was exhausted and ready to go home, but she still had to transfer her possessions from what was now Agnes's domain to Steve Novak's old place of business.

And the first thing I'm getting rid of is that strip of grandiose red carpet, she thought gleefully as she dumped an armload of files on to her chair. 'Nobody's going to think of *me* as the Queen of Sheba.'

She didn't realise she was talking out loud until Clayte's voice remarked from the doorway, 'I don't think there's much danger of that. The Queen of Sheba didn't wear beige linen business suits, to my knowledge. Very appropriate, by the way. A great improvement on the black overall.'

'Perhaps you should consider dressing your house-keeping staff in beige business suits, then,' retorted Georgina, who was tired of his gibes about her clothes.

'I'll think about it.' He glanced at his watch. 'Dinner at eight tonight, if you don't mind. I have a couple of things to do first.'

Georgina sat down heavily on the files which she'd dumped on her chair. 'Thank you, but I can't have dinner with you tonight,' she said firmly. 'I have other plans.'

'Do you now? Were you planning to wash walls or shake the cushions?' He bent over her with his palms spread flat on her blotter, and to her horror she experienced a *frisson* of undiluted physical need such as she hadn't felt for a very long time.

She leaned back in an effort to escape the spell she suspected he knew he was casting. 'I was planning to have my—my neighbours over for dinner,' she replied as coldly as possible. 'I'd ask you too, but I'm afraid I've already baked an apple pie.'

She felt a momentary thrill of triumph when she saw a startled look pass over his face. Then his eyes deepened, and he laughed softly. 'Nice one, Georgina. And don't worry. Neighbourly dinners aren't really my style.'

Somehow, without even trying, he'd managed to make her feel like a dowdy little homebody again. She stood up, and half a dozen files tumbled on to the floor. 'I didn't think they were,' she said, smiling sweetly, and wondering what Clayte would say if he knew that her neighbours happened to be her ex-husband and his wife. She didn't intend to find out. Her social life, such as it was, was none of his business.

'Goodnight, Mr O'Neill,' she said, holding out her hand and reverting to non-threatening formality. 'I'll see you in the morning, I expect.'

He took her outstretched fingers and held on to them just a shade longer than necessary. 'I expect you will, Mrs Kettrick,' he said equably. 'By the way, I hope you looked after my air-conditioning?'

Georgina noted that he too had reverted to formality, and some devil in her made her reply, 'Of course I did. A good night's sleep should do wonders for your disposition.' She bent down to pick up the spilled files without waiting for him to respond. But when she stood up he was still there, standing with one hand in his pocket while the fingers of the other strummed rhythmically against her new desk. She was embarrassingly aware that he'd been studying her posterior with interest.

'Are you actively *looking* for trouble?' he enquired curiously. 'If so, I can certainly arrange it.'

To her annoyance, Georgina found herself clutching the back of her chair. 'No,' she said irritably. 'I'm looking for Michael's supply list. It seems to have—oh, here it is.' She pulled a sheet of paper from the top file and made a great production of spreading it out on her desk.

'Lucky for you,' said Clayte cryptically. 'Don't forget, if you want trouble, I'll be happy to oblige. I'm an expert. Goodnight, Georgina.'

Before she could form more than a startled, 'Goodnight,' he had spun on his heel and was already striding out of the door.

She watched his tall figure disappear with a reluctant little tug of admiration, and wondered how soon he would leave Snowlake. Whenever it was, it couldn't be too soon. And thank God for Gordon and Isabel. If it hadn't been for them, she would have been hard-pressed to avoid Clayte's invitation.

Funny, never in a million years would she have expected Gordon and his second wife to become her friends. But they had.

Ten years ago her ex-husband had shattered her dreams of a happy home and family when he announced one bright April morning that he had come to the conclusion that he wasn't suited to marriage. She had been crushed, totally devastated and lost. But the pain had healed, she had learned to deal with life on her own terms, and when she'd walked into the Snowlake real estate office six months ago and discovered that Gordon was the current owner she had been able to greet him without pain and as an old and kindly remembered friend.

He had put on weight in the years since she had last seen him. He looked well-padded, well-heeled, and utterly different from the feckless young husband who had wanted to spend money they didn't have on parties, bars and fast motorcycles, while she toiled away cleaning houses and trying to save for a future that never came.

It turned out that four years ago he had met Isabel, and overnight exchanged parties for pigeons, which he and his wife bred for racing with a great deal of love and devotion.

When Gordon, perhaps out of guilt, had suggested that the cottage a few hundred yards from his own house might just suit her she had been doubtful. More than doubtful. She had put the divorce behind her, but, even so, if it hadn't been for Gordon's desertion, by now she might be a mother, instead of a woman rising thirty who even now couldn't see herself with another man. Then she'd seen the cottage and met Isabel, his short-necked, exuberant young wife. The cottage was her dream home. And down-to-earth Isabel had put her mind at rest within two minutes of their first awkward meeting.

'Worry about you and Gordon?' she had laughed. 'Of course not. Why should I? I've seen the way you two look at each other.'

'Er—how's that?'

'Sort of friendly, but bewildered. As though you can't see why you ever felt attracted.'

As that about summed it up, a month later Georgina had moved into the cottage. Gordon sometimes fixed recalcitrant plumbing for her, and Isabel became the close friend her peripatetic childhood had never allowed her to make. She supposed it was an unusual arrangement, but it worked.

Sighing for no particular reason, Georgina began to put away the files.

Two days later, apparently satisfied that his hotel wouldn't fall apart under her management, Clayte marched into the bar, where she was discussing new seating with Harvey, and announced that he was returning to Los Angeles in the morning.

'And tonight I won't take no for an answer,' he informed her when he'd broken the news.

Georgina pulled down the bottom of her tailored suit jacket and stood up straight, as Harvey, looking embarrassed, scuttled quickly behind the polished mahogany bar.

'I'm not your type,' she said coolly.

Clayte's eyebrows shot up. Then after a moment a malicious grin sharpened his features. 'Ah, yes,' he said. 'I'd forgotten. You're not a service provided by this hotel.'

She stared at him, determined not to betray her confusion, and suddenly he lifted his shoulders and said in a much more friendly tone, 'Don't worry, Georgina, I was inviting you out to dinner, not into my bed. I haven't much use for men who blackmail their female employees.'

'Oh,' said Georgina, caught off guard. And then, recovering quickly, 'I should hope not. And I'm afraid——'

'That you can't make dinner? Think again, Mrs Kettrick. You can. You and I still have a lot to discuss.'

Georgina sank down into the nearest red leather chair and thought fast. It was probable that he did have more instructions and orders to give her. He'd been full of them for the past few days. But she wasn't anxious for a repeat of the episode on the dance-floor—and she already had a chicken thawing in her fridge. As Clayte had indicated that home cooking was anathema to him, it was a safe bet that if she invited him to dinner he would refuse.

'If it's essential,' she said, crossing her slim legs and looking up at him, 'I can provide you with dinner at my place. It's already thawed. If that doesn't suit you, I'm afraid we'll have to conduct our business here.'

'Hmm.' Clayte frowned, his thick brows looking more devilish than ever. 'I warn you, Georgina, if this is some kind of domestic trap...'

'Trap?' said Georgina, standing up again. 'Why should I want to trap *you*?'

He let out a crack of laughter. 'There's not much danger of my getting above myself in your company, is there? All right, I'll accept your offer. It seems I have no other choice.'

'Thanks,' said Georgina. 'You don't do a lot for *my* ego either, if that makes you feel any better. As it happens I'm a very good cook.'

Clayte groaned. 'I was afraid you might be.'

'What is it with you?' she asked, irritated. 'I know you go for the sophisticated lifestyle, but there's nothing wrong with decent, home-cooked food. It won't poison you, and as I have no designs on your delectable body I don't see why you're making such a fuss.'

'Am I making a fuss? My apologies. And I have no objection to designs on my—did you say delectable?— body.'

She had, but she certainly hadn't meant to. 'Slip of the tongue,' she said, exasperated by the taunting slant of his mouth. 'You can come over any time after seven-thirty. I have to finish up here first.'

'Dismissed again,' said Clayte with an exaggerated sigh. 'Bear in mind, Mrs Kettrick, that if I choose to I have the right to dismiss you.'

'I'm well aware of it,' said Georgina, walking away from him and going over to talk to Harvey, who was wiping the same spot on the counter for the fourth time in as many minutes. 'I'll see you later, *Mr* O'Neill.'

After Clayte left, Harvey smiled at her and tossed his bushy head at the door. 'Bossy so-and-so, isn't he?' he commented.

'Yes,' agreed Georgina, 'I suppose that's because he is the boss.'

Harvey shuffled his feet, and Georgina felt contrite. The trouble with being manager was that it wasn't politic to criticise the boss in front of staff with whom only a week ago she would have shared a satisfactory grumble.

She was still brooding about her changed status when Clayte arrived at the cottage shortly before eight, bearing a very good bottle of chilled champagne. Georgina eyed it warily. He caught the look and said impatiently, 'For heaven's sake, Georgina, it's a gift, not the preliminary to a night of seduction. If it's any comfort to you, I never conduct seductions when I'm wearing a suit because, like you, I never mix business with pleasure.'

Oh, so that was why he'd arrived at her unpretentious home to eat at her kitchen table dressed as if they were about to arrange a corporate merger. She was wearing a plain blue blouse and trousers. They made her feel a bit like Cinderella when the prince came to try on the slipper. But if she changed it would be obvious that she felt at a disadvantage. Clayte had enough of an upper hand as it was. A hand which, she was reluctantly obliged to admit as she watched him sprawl elegantly against the arm of her sofa, she wouldn't altogether mind on certain parts of her. It had been too long...

Thank goodness he was leaving tomorrow.

Clayte was as good as his word. The evening was strictly business and very little pleasure. They discussed budgets, personnel and suppliers, and he consumed her beautifully crisp chicken as if he thought he was doing her a favour. Later, when she brought him his coffee, he watched her clear the table with a cynical little smile on his lips.

'Would you like to help me with the dishes?' she asked, goaded beyond discretion by the smile. Normally she refused to let guests come anywhere near her kitchen sink.

'No,' he said. 'I don't do dishes. That's what I employ a housekeeper for. Now, as our business seems to be concluded, and I have an early flight coming up in the morning, I think it's time I headed back to the Inn.'

'Yes, of course,' said Georgina, surprised to find that she felt a quick stab of regret. 'Thanks for the champagne.'

'My pleasure.' He stood up, and she followed him over to the door.

He opened it to the warm July dusk, and for a moment Georgina thought he didn't even mean to say goodnight. But when he reached the top step he turned suddenly. His face was only a few inches above hers.

'Well, Georgina,' he said softly. 'It's been—interesting. Thank you.'

She nodded, her mouth suddenly parched. She could see the pores of his skin and a faint shadow darkening his jawline. And in his eyes was a look she hadn't seen there before. He was gazing at her upturned face as if he saw something there that shocked him, something he didn't want to see. Then he muttered a word under his breath that sounded to her like, 'Damnation.'

'What is it?' she asked, forcing herself not to whisper. There was no need to, but for some reason she felt a sense of danger, as if noise might bring disaster crashing around them.

He shook his head and didn't answer. Then, as she made to step backwards, he raised his hand and drew a finger very slowly across her cheek. Involuntarily, she gasped, as desire, hot and undeniable, flared in the pit of her stomach and shivered down to her toes. Clayte smiled, a twisted, all-too-knowing smile, and the spell was broken.

'Not a chance, Georgina,' he said, sounding unaccountably tired. 'I'm wearing a suit, remember?' His smile changed, became rueful and strangely self-mocking. Inexplicably, it made her want to put her arms around him. Instead she stepped back.

Clayte's eyes met hers in sardonic understanding. 'I'll be in touch,' he said carelessly, and strode away down the path. But when he reached the gate he turned back and added in a very businesslike voice, 'Don't forget, guests of the Willow Inn have high standards. I don't tolerate inefficiency at any time.'

Before Georgina could tell him that she didn't tolerate rude and dictatorial men, he had swung his supple body into one of the Inn's sleek silver sedans, and was manoeuvring it round a bend in the road.

She backed slowly into the house and closed the door. Another extraordinary evening, she thought dazedly. But then Clayte was an extraordinary man. Not just because he had risen from the ranks to become the owner of a hotel empire, but because he was such an unusual and complex individual.

As Georgina headed into the kitchen to do the dishes
he'd declined to help with, she wondered what had
caused his almost violent antipathy to the traditional
skills that most men valued in a woman. It couldn't be
just his way of avoiding the tender trap. Or could it?
With Clayte you never knew. At least, she didn't. And
what was more she didn't care, she reminded herself.
The two of them wanted totally different things, and his
interest in her, of course, had been strictly business.

Had been. He'd gone, and wasn't likely to be back.
Unless she made a royal mess of things, in which case
he might return to dismiss her.

Pulling a face at her reflection in the window,
Georgina picked up his empty coffee-cup and dumped
it into the sink.

'Mrs Kettrick, where the hell do you think you've been?'

Georgina gasped as she hurried through the polished
front doors into the oak-beamed lobby of the Inn.
Clayte's roar of outrage burst over her like exploding
shrapnel. He had been striding past the reception desk
when she entered, but the moment he saw her he stopped
dead to deliver his blast.

She closed her eyes. It wasn't possible. Clayte had been
gone from the hotel for a week. But she wasn't subject
to visions, and there had been nothing illusory about
that voice.

She raised her eyelids cautiously. Yes, it was Clayte
all right. Glowering, furious and with one clenched fist
resting on the counter.

'Well?' he demanded, in control still, but only barely.
'I'm waiting for an answer, Mrs Kettrick.'

Oh, lord, why did he have to look so sexy, even when
he was in a towering rage? 'I—I've been feeding my

neighbours' pigeons,' replied Georgina hastily. 'And exercising them. They've won so many races this season that Isabel and Gordon have decided they owe themselves a bit of a celebration. They've gone to Reno for a couple of days.'

'I don't care where they've gone. You're paid to run my hotel, not feed pigeons.' Clayte detached himself from the counter and came towards her, very much in charge of his world. 'Follow me,' he said peremptorily.

Georgina followed him. She didn't want the entire staff to hear her raked over the coals by her irate employer, and Lori already looked as if she was settling down to enjoy a good scene.

Clayte led her into her own office. 'Shut the door,' he ordered.

She shut it.

'Right.' He rested a hand on the wall above her shoulder. 'Now tell me why the devil you were feeding pigeons on *my* time, when you were supposed to be here running this hotel.'

Georgina licked her lips. 'It wasn't your time,' she replied, as calmly as possible. 'It was my time. I'm entitled to have lunch, I believe.'

'Not at...' he glanced at his watch, '...not at four-fifteen in the afternoon, you're not.'

'I didn't take time off earlier,' she explained tightly. 'The birds are always fed and exercised around four. And the Inn manages to run itself very nicely without my twenty-four-hour presence in this office.'

'Mrs Kettrick.' His voice was low and dangerous, and Georgina wished he would move away. 'Mrs Kettrick, I don't know about you, but I wouldn't say a kitchen without a chef was running nicely. Chef Alexander has just walked out. We are putting on a banquet for eighty guests this evening, so I'm informed. What do you propose we should feed them? Georgina Kettrick's home-cooked chicken and biscuits? I understand they've ordered baked salmon. With Alexander's famous mustard cream sauce.'

CHAPTER FOUR

GEORGINA'S mouth fell open before she could prevent it. 'Chef Alexander has walked out?' she repeated stupidly. 'You mean he's quit?'

'That's what I said.'

'Oh. But why?'

'You tell me. I'm not an expert on the care and feeding of Alexander. *You're* supposed to be in charge here, Georgina.'

Oh, so she was Georgina again. But it didn't make much difference. He was pronouncing her name as if it left an unpleasant taste in his mouth.

'All right,' she said. 'If you'll move out of my way, I'll go and check with the kitchen.'

'The kitchen,' he replied, 'is in an uproar. They're running around in there like a bunch of brain-damaged chickens. Or will *pigeons* get the point across better?'

'The point is taken.' She glared into his aggressively set face. 'But I can't do much about it until you move.'

Instead of moving, Clayte put his free hand on the other side of her head so that she was trapped against the wall with his powerful body blocking her escape. She felt a sudden surge of heat that had nothing to do with the temperature in the room.

For a few seconds he just stood there, glaring at her, and she found herself staring at the hard outline of his lips. They parted, showing a glimpse of his teeth, and for one incredible moment she thought he meant to kiss her.

She shut her eyes, with the crazy thought that if she couldn't see what was happening it wouldn't happen. When she opened them again, he had moved away.

'OK,' he said, jerking his head at the door. 'Get on with it.'

Georgina frowned. He thought she couldn't do it—wouldn't be able to cope with this crisis. Stifling an impulse to tell him in explicit detail exactly where he could stuff his rotten job, she spun round and made her way back to the lobby.

Lori took one look at her face and clamped her mouth shut—for which minor mercy Georgina supposed she ought to feel grateful. Then she glanced up and saw Mrs Durham approaching, and only just managed to refrain from groaning out loud.

'Mrs Kettrick,' quivered the anxious voice of one of the hotel's least popular and most frequent guests, 'I can't seem to find my husband. Do you——?'

'I'm afraid I haven't seen him, Mrs Durham.' Georgina flashed the twittery little woman her public-relations smile and dodged round her before she could start explaining when, where and why she had managed to mislay Mr Durham, who was a political figure of some note. His wife was a chronic worrier and complainer, who kept the whole staff in a state of agitated uproar with her constant fussing.

In view of her assurance to Clayte, Georgina was determined that for the next hour the kitchen would be her only priority.

Clayte. Vaguely, as she hurried towards the sound of raised voices, it occurred to her to wonder how she could have been dim-witted enough to regret her employer's absence this past week. Because the truth was, she had missed him. Actually missed him. She should have had brains enough to know when she was well off.

It wasn't until she reached the big, modern kitchen that contrasted so starkly with the old-fashioned ambience of the Inn that Georgina became aware that the cause of her irritation was right behind her. In fact his hand was on the small of her back.

She took in the scene at a glance. Chaos, just as she had expected, was running amok. Carlos, the moustached first cook, was desperately trying to restore calm amid a steamy atmosphere of heat and panic. Georgina sympathised with his predicament. Alexander had ruled the kitchen with an iron hand in which the reins of command had always been tightly controlled. Alexander did *not* delegate, and without his autocratic but masterly supervision Carlos had only a very shaky idea of what to do. And Carlos had never had the head chef's culinary brilliance. He was a competent plodder, but no more.

By this time on a normal day Alexander would have been flitting from work station to work station, tasting this, prodding that, and screaming at some unfortunate minion that there was too much vinegar in the salad dressing, and not enough salt in the sauce. Today, although the kitchen was bustling with mindless activity, very little was actually getting done. And half the floor seemed to be covered with some sort of congealing brown liquid, which Matthew, the pot-washer, was heroically trying to clean up.

'What happened?' asked Georgina, halting them all in mid-panic as she stopped just inside the door with the assumption of a confidence she didn't feel. Clayte's hand was still on her back, and she stepped forward to avoid what she suspected was an attempt to remind her who was boss. As if she could possibly forget!

Carlos held out his hands, palms extended, and rolled up his eyes. 'Alexander, he comes in growling. I think he had fight with his wife. Then fish comes. Looks good fish to me, but Alexander says no, no good. Nothing any good. Then Basil, he try to lift stock pot. Drops it. Basil burns hand, Mr O'Neill comes in, takes Basil to hospital——'

'How is he?' asked Georgina quickly.

'He'll live.' Clayte's voice behind her cracked with impatience. 'But he won't be working tonight.'

'Oh, dear,' murmured Georgina. 'What happened then, Carlos?'

Carlos affected a sudden interest in the ceiling. 'We get on with dinner. Mr O'Neill, he comes back, tells Alexander he shouldn't allow accident to happen. Alexander makes noise like sick engine. Phone rings. Wholesaler say payment late, so no delivery tomorrow——'

'Payment? What payment?'

The first cook shrugged, and somewhere at the back of the room a pan hit the floor with a clatter. Georgina jumped. 'What payment, Carlos? All our invoices were paid on time.'

Carlos shrugged again. 'Don't know. Miss Duncan, she not know either.' He removed his gaze from the ceiling and fixed it on the floor. 'She say maybe new manager make muddle. Alexander, he throw hands in air, say many English words. Stamp foot. Marie—she new kitchen helper—she giggle. Alexander say, "OK, very funny, I quit". Takes off apron, walks out.'

'All right,' said Georgina, who was beginning to see a little light. 'Thank you, Carlos, that was a very helpful explanation. I suggest you handle things as best you can, then.' She glanced round the chaotic kitchen. 'Better get that asparagus washed, but you're doing fine. And I'll see what I can do about Alexander.'

'Impressive, Mrs Kettrick,' said Clayte's harsh voice from behind her. 'Handled with diplomacy and tact.'

As Georgina began to turn towards him, astounded by the unexpected praise, he added caustically, 'There's just one small problem, though, isn't there? Alexander has no intention of coming back.'

'No. Not come back,' agreed Carlos, glumly shaking his head.

'Oh, I think he will.' Georgina pasted a smile on her face. She didn't really think anything of the sort, but she was on her mettle now, rising to Clayte's unspoken challenge. If anyone could get Alexander to return to his post, she meant to be the one to do it.

'Perhaps you'd like to take over in the kitchen,' she said to Clayte, taking pleasure in the look of disbelieving astonishment he threw at her as she turned her back. She made straight for her office and at once picked up the intercom to ask Lori to put Miss Duncan on the line.

A wary voice answered, 'Hello?'

'Miss Duncan,' she said abruptly. 'What's this nonsense about an invoice not being paid?'

There was a long pause. 'Um—I'm not sure, Georgina. Perhaps it got lost in the mail.'

Georgina's eyes narrowed, and she began to rifle through her outgoing mail tray. At the very bottom, casually concealed beneath a sheet of plain white paper, was the missing payment.

'And perhaps, Miss Duncan,' she said with icy control, 'you removed it from the outgoing mail in the hopes of putting me out of a job. I realise you haven't been able to accept me in place of Mr Novak, but that hardly excuses outright disloyalty.'

There was another pause, and then Miss Duncan's hostile voice said, 'Well, if you're going to start accusing me of lying, I'll have to——'

'Quit? Good. I was about to suggest it. You'll be paid till the end of the month.'

She put down the receiver with a snap, and looked up to see Clayte leaning against the panelling, watching her. His dark eyes were very bright and piercing, and his lips were slanted up in speculation.

'Well, well,' he said. 'Mrs Kettrick takes no prisoners, I see.'

'Miss Duncan is very well qualified. She'll have no trouble finding another job,' Georgina snapped. She was in no mood to put up with Clayte's sniping.

'Are you sure she's guilty?'

'Quite sure. There have been other, less damaging incidents which I unwisely chose to overlook. But I can no longer put up with an assistant who engages in sabotage.'

'I agree,' said Clayte. 'On the other hand, if you don't do something about the kitchen, you may not have to put up with any kind of assistant.'

'Is that a threat?'

'No. A warning.'

Georgina frowned. She had an odd sensation that in spite of his concern about the chef Clayte was enjoying himself. Like a cat who enjoyed tormenting a mouse. Some cat, she thought involuntarily. More like a sabre-toothed tiger. And she wasn't going to give him a chance to pounce.

But she *was* going to solve the problem in the kitchen even if it meant kidnapping Alexander at gunpoint. Not that she owned a gun, or wanted to, but it was a pleasing fantasy.

Ignoring Clayte, who was now perched on the edge of her desk with one polished black shoe resting on her plant-stand, Georgina punched briskly at the keyboard of her computer. When it came up with Alexander's address, she scribbled it on a piece of paper and announced without looking at her employer that she would report back to him in an hour or less.

'Less,' he responded tersely, causing Georgina to press her lips together.

Alexander lived in a big, airy house halfway up the hill above the lake. He greeted her at the door with a scowl, an exuberant Airedale and a grudging invitation to, 'Come in.' The dog, whose name was Rajah, greeted her by placing two monstrous paws on her shoulders and toppling her on to her back.

Half an hour later, as Georgina drove back the way she had come, she was smiling broadly and humming 'We Shall Overcome' under her breath. Who would have thought that an Airedale would turn out to be a useful bargaining chip?

When she arrived at the Willow Inn, at first glance everything seemed normal, which was obviously too good to be true. 'Where is Mr O'Neill?' she asked warily. 'Baring his fangs in the kitchen?'

Lori giggled, and Georgina remembered guiltily that managers weren't supposed to make critical remarks about their bosses.

'No, he's in his room, I think,' said the receptionist. 'Would you like me to check?'

'I suppose so,' she agreed doubtfully, remembering that the last time she had disturbed Clayte by phone he'd been about as civilised as a hungry tiger in pursuit of breakfast. But she had promised to get back to him within the hour, and there wasn't much likelihood that he'd be sleeping. Not this time. That was just the trouble.

'Yes,' she said, more positively. 'You'd better check. Thanks.'

Lori dialled Clayte's number, and handed the phone to Georgina.

'Who is it?' he snapped.

She lifted her eyebrows. Apparently the tiger hadn't caught his prey. 'It's Mrs Kettrick,' she said, very pointedly. 'I thought you'd want to know——'

'I do. Come on up, Georgina.' He sounded slightly less abrasive now, but it was obvious that he was trying to control the urge to snap.

'To your room?' she enquired icily. 'I hardly think——'

'Don't worry, I'm decent this time. I'm also in the middle of shaving, so could you please suppress the maidenly blushes and get up here?'

'Very well, Mr O'Neill,' replied Georgina, hoping Lori hadn't caught the drift of the conversation. 'I'll be with you shortly.'

She hung up before he could tell her shortly wouldn't do. Then she made her way speedily to the kitchen, where the floor was clean but the atmosphere only slightly less frantic and steamy than before.

'How's it going, Carlos?' she asked, in a power-of-positive-thinking sort of voice.

'Asparagus clean,' he said quickly.

Well, that was something. Leaving him with further instructions to keep up the good work, and assurances that help was on the way, Georgina went upstairs to face Clayte.

He was in Room 23 again. When he answered her knock, he was wearing navy trousers and a white shirt open at the neck. It occurred to Georgina that apart from that one occasion when she had encountered him wearing next to nothing this was only the second time she had seen him in anything less than full executive-hunk uniform. His face was smoother than usual and slightly damp. He looked healthy, sexy and mouth-wateringly male.

She opened her mouth, closed it again, and tried very hard not to gulp. He said nothing, but stood looking down at her with his legs apart and one hand on each side of the door.

'I thought I'd find you in the kitchen bullying the staff,' she said finally. His silence and his crude virility were starting to get on her nerves.

'I was, until young Matthew—he'll go far, that boy— had the gumption to take me aside and point out that if I didn't get the hell out of there Carlos would likely quit as well. Or use me as the base for a fresh stockpot.'

Georgina, unable to resist the wry self-derision in his eyes, gave a low gurgle of laughter. This was a side of Clayte she hadn't seen before. He could actually laugh at himself. 'You're very courageous,' she told him. 'I didn't think you'd ever admit the possibility that your presence could be anything less than inspirational.'

Clayte acknowledged the barb with a look that was less than reassuring. 'It had nothing to do with courage,' he informed her, 'and a lot to do with plain common sense. I can't see where the Willow Inn's reputation would be well-served by undercooked fish, overcooked vegetables and cold soup.'

'With you as the base? I should think not.' Georgina eyed him pensively. His voice still had that hard edge to it, but he didn't seem as belligerent as before.

'You needn't worry,' she said, after a moment's reflection, and with what she considered was permissable smugness. 'Alexander's on his way back. It'll be a close call, but he says he can get dinner on the tables on time.'

Clayte stopped blocking the door and stepped back. 'Come in, Georgina,' he said, waving at the room behind him. 'You're beginning to interest me. No, not that sort of interest,' he scoffed, when he saw her eyes widen with alarm.

Annoyingly, aside from wishing that she hadn't given her thoughts away, Georgina felt a jab of disappointment—and then felt angry with herself for feeling it. She waited until an elderly couple had gone into their room before walking past Clayte with her head high, and sitting down primly on the red velvet chair beneath the window. The last time she had seen this particular chair it had been decorated by Clayte's white bath-towel.

He swung into the room and closed the door, his movements economical and smooth. When Georgina saw the purposeful way he was rolling back his shirt-cuffs, she crossed her legs and gazed quickly out of the window. A small boat with red sails was bobbing about on the lake, and she fixed her eyes on it with flustered concentration.

'OK,' said Clayte, dropping on to the bed and lying back with a complete lack of self-consciousness, 'how did you do it?'

Georgina removed her gaze from the boat. 'Well, to start with, Alexander's Airedale ran me over.'

Clayte linked his hands behind his head, and settled himself more comfortably on the pillow. 'A promising beginning,' he murmured sceptically.

'It was, as a matter of fact.' Georgina tried not to notice the enticing pull of the fabric across his thighs. 'I collected a couple of bruises, and Alexander was sure I meant to sue.'

'And did you? Mean to sue?'

'No, of course not. What's a bruise or two between friends? But it put Alexander in a more accommodating mood than he might have been otherwise. And I promised him I'd make sure his delivery arrived on schedule tomorrow if I had to take the cheque in myself. He liked that. And when I told him you were very sorry for saying the accident with the stockpot was his fault—— '

'I'm not in the least sorry. He was in charge.'

'Well, don't tell him that, or he'll quit again. The kitchen staff are doing their best, but it won't be good enough without Alexander.'

Clayte closed his eyes. 'Are you telling me how to run my hotel, Georgina Kettrick?'

Georgina watched the dark lashes fan out across his cheeks, and swallowed hastily. 'No,' she said. 'You can run it any way you like. But if you want to see dinner on the tables this evening you'd better control the over-powering need you have to throw your weight around and manage people.'

'All right. I'll concentrate on managing you.' His lazy drawl unaccountably made her feel warm.

'No, you won't,' she said hastily. 'I've been inde-pendent for too long to be any good at taking orders. So has Alexander. Although when I told him how desperately he was missed he agreed very quickly to come back. I think he wanted to really.'

'No doubt. He's extremely well-paid. And I suppose you offered him a raise?'

She shook her head. 'No. I didn't need to.'

Clayte lifted sleepy-looking eyelids and shot her a look that was remarkably perceptive for a man who appeared on the verge of slumber.

'I really *am* impressed,' he said softly. 'Well done, Georgina.'

To her horror, Georgina found herself blushing. 'It— it wasn't difficult,' she mumbled, wondering why on earth words of praise from this man should have the effect of turning her into a stuttering adolescent. She certainly didn't stutter when he shouted at her—she answered back. 'Even you could have done it,' she added, sitting up very straight and smoothing her hand over the red velvet.

'Yes. And I *would* have done it if necessary. But my methods would have been rather different from yours.'

'I know. A mixture of blackmail, bribery and sheer bossiness. But you'd have got your way.'

Clayte gave a surprisingly bitter laugh and sat up suddenly, swinging his long legs off the bed so that once again her gaze was drawn to their elegant length. 'So that's what you think of me,' he muttered. 'Well, you may be right. And I apologise for taking my frustrations out on you.'

She wondered what particular frustrations he was referring to, but happily had the good sense not to ask. 'It doesn't matter,' she said. 'You had a right to expect me to be here.'

'True. And the pigeons hadn't. All the same...' He paused, and a reflective look came into his eyes. 'All the same, you've proved yourself a capable manager. I'd no right to shout at you——'

'Why not? It's a habit of yours, isn't it?'

He frowned. 'It's also a habit of mine to make amends for my occasional lapses.'

Occasional! thought Georgina. Who does he think he's kidding? For some reason Clayte's overwhelming confidence was getting under her skin more than it usually did today. 'I suppose,' she said without thinking, 'that your idea of amends is a kiss and a dozen red roses.'

To her consternation, Clayte grinned outrageously and at once stood up and held out his hand. 'Yellow roses,' he said. 'But you've got the kiss part right. Come here.'

Georgina's heart skidded to a halt. '*Mr* O'Neill!' she exclaimed, doing her best to sound like the heroine's imposing great-aunt in an improbable Restoration comedy. '*Mr* O'Neill, I'll thank you to remember that I'm your employee.'

'I know. So come here.'

Georgina put a hand on the arm of her chair and stood up awkwardly, keeping a wary eye on the narrow space in between Clayte's body and the door. 'You assured me that kissing your managers isn't something you do,' she said indignantly. 'You said it was bad for morale.'

'Uh-huh. And would it be bad for your morale, Georgina?'

She stared at him, mesmerised by the glint in his eyes. Was he serious? He couldn't be. And yes, it would be incredibly bad for her morale. Devastating, in fact. No woman could be proof against the potent sensuality of this man—and she knew she was no exception. Had known all along. She didn't have to *like* Clayton O'Neill to be susceptible to his magnetic sensuality. And the last thing she needed at this stage in her life was to fall for a man whose priorities were the very antithesis of her own. A man who loathed comfortable domesticity almost as much as she loved it. A man to whom roots were a lead weight instead of a safe anchor from the storm.

'Yes,' she said flatly. 'It would be extremely bad for my morale. And very unethical on your part.' She started to make a move towards the door, but the moment she drew level with him he caught her elbow.

'You're right,' he said, gazing into her eyes with a curiously guarded expression, as if he had just received a shock and didn't want anyone to know. 'It would be unethical. But kisses only count as harassment when they're unwelcome.'

Georgina gulped, unbearably conscious of the warm pressure of his hand through her linen suit, her gaze riveted on the full curve of the parted lips that were altogether too near to her own. Dear lord, his kiss wouldn't be unwelcome. It would merely be fatal.

She took a deep breath and said, 'Please let me go.'

He did so at once. 'Right.' His briskness appalled her. 'Kisses are out. How about roses?'

Georgina tried to smile and couldn't quite manage it. 'My house is covered in yellow roses,' she said quietly.

'So it is. All right, then, since you've succeeded in pulling Alexander out of your hat for me, how about we sample his speciality, and then head out for a night on the town?'

'There's not much town to head out for,' she pointed out. 'And we've already been to the Pelican. Besides, I don't expect to be wined and dined just because I happened to do my job.'

Clayte sighed. 'Do you practise it, Georgina, or does it come naturally?'

'What?' She blinked at him, and took another quick step towards the door.

'Being difficult. I *want* to take you out, you impossible woman. I owe you one, I'd rather not eat alone, and——'

'And you always get your own way.' She gave him a vinegary little smile and turned away.

Before she reached the door he was behind her, his strong hands firm on her shoulders. 'Yes,' he said, pulling her back until she could feel his lean length all along her spine, 'I try to. And I'm getting it this time. Do you want to change? If not, that sensible beige you're wearing will do quite well. On you it looks almost seductive.'

Help! His flattering words were having the disastrous effect of making her want to turn around, throw her arms about him and press herself against the supple body that was already doing such stimulating things to her back. But she mustn't do it. And she'd already been in his room far too long. Lori might notice.

Clayte was rubbing his thumb gently along the base of her neck. 'OK?' he asked. 'Objections over and done with?'

They weren't, by a long shot. But to her amazement she heard herself saying, 'Yes, OK. I won't bother to change, if you don't mind.'

'I don't mind.'

'I expect you'll find me in the kitchen,' she hurried on, flustered by the sensuous purr of his voice. 'I want to make sure everything's under control.'

'That's what I like to see,' said Clayte approvingly, 'my managers busy on the job. Not feeding pigeons.'

Georgina gritted her teeth and opened the door. As he closed it behind her, his low chuckle followed her all the way down the oak-panelled hall.

In the kitchen, calm was by no means restored, and Alexander's temper under the added pressure was even more volatile than usual. But the salmon was ready to bake, the pastry cook was stirring dough instead of tearing his hair out and groaning, and Carlos was smiling with relief under the familiar stream of Alexander's abuse.

Yes, dinner would be ready on time.

Later, with the banquet proceeding smoothly in a separate part of the hotel, Clayte and Georgina took their places in what should have been a discreet corner of the dining-room. It wasn't discreet enough, though, and Georgina found the curious glances of the staff very unsettling.

'If Alexander saw you pecking at his food like that, he'd be very hurt,' Clayte reproved her, as he tucked in with the enthusiasm of a natural athlete whose body needed substantial stoking.

'I know,' said Georgina, sampling a small spoonful of *crème caramel*. She sighed. 'Doesn't it bother you that everyone's trying to pretend they can't actually see us? And that the busboy has set the table next to us three times in the past ten minutes?'

Clayte laughed softly. 'No, it doesn't bother me in the least. Should it?'

'I suppose not. You own this hotel, and you'll be leaving. I won't, and if people think I'm—well, that I got the job by——'

'Sleeping your way to the top?' he suggested. 'I don't think you need worry about that.'

'I wasn't,' she said, aghast. And did he mean that she needn't worry about sleeping with him, or that people weren't likely to think it? Either way, it wasn't exactly flattering.

'Weren't you? Then what *is* worrying you?' Clayte brought her back to her original comment.

'I don't know. You are, I suppose,' she admitted honestly.

He arched his thick eyebrows deliberately. 'Am I?' he purred. 'What a very promising remark.'

Georgina put down her coffee-cup. It rattled a bit against the saucer. 'Clayte, can we go now?'

He smiled in that superior way she was sure he knew particularly annoyed her, and rose to his feet without even bothering to answer.

Fifteen minutes later they were seated in the hotel sedan driving swiftly down the highway to the border.

'Hey! Where are we going?' demanded Georgina when she realised that Snowlake was behind them.

'Vancouver. As you pointed out, apart from several overcrowded bars and a couple of honky-tonk night-clubs, the nightlife in Snowlake is more or less limited to the Pelican—which we've already done.'

'Yes, but I don't need nightlife. I'm quite happy to——'

'Sit at home and knit?' he suggested. 'I don't doubt it. I suppose you sew too. Lumpy little numbers with "home-made" written all over them.'

'Yes,' said Georgina through her teeth, and wondering what had caused him to turn all biting and cynical again. 'I do knit. And sew. I happen to enjoy it. And my little numbers are *not* lumpy. What is it with you, Clayte? Why are you always taking aim at activities that give *me* great pleasure? I don't sneer at you because you like nightlife and dancing and—and——'

'Fast cars and fast women?' he finished for her. 'Oh, those aren't my only interests, my dear. I also like sailing and heli-skiing and tennis——'

'Fine,' snapped Georgina. 'Well, *I* like cooking and sewing and knitting and—and *pigeons*.'

'Pigeons!' Clayte threw his head back and roared with laughter. The window was open, and the wind ruffling through his thick black hair made him look wild, dangerous and exotic. Georgina dug her nails into her palms and glared, tight-lipped, at the flat landscape hurtling past the window.

'There's nothing funny about pigeons,' she muttered finally. 'They're fascinating. Even now, nobody knows what triggers their homing instinct. And pigeons have been war heroes too, for carrying messages across enemy lines and getting killed and wounded for their trouble——' She broke off, because for some reason her throat was becoming all choked.

Clayte turned to look at her, but she didn't see his laughter sober into a frown, or the way his leather-clad fingers tightened over the wheel. When he spoke, though, she heard the change in his voice.

'Georgina,' he said, as if he were patiently explaining the obvious to a child, 'if it makes a difference, I really don't dislike pigeons. And it's not you I'm taking aim at particularly. What you choose to do with your spare time doesn't concern me. It's just that I can't stand to see an intelligent woman wasting her time on domestic trivialities. I've nothing against cleanliness, but when the home becomes an obsession, when all a woman can think of is new curtains, the whiteness of her wash, and whether her kitchen floor is as shiny as the next door neighbour's——'

'I'm not like that,' Georgina protested.

'No, perhaps not, because you've been too busy earning a living. But just give you a chance—a husband with an income—— '

'I had a husband.'

'Sure, but no income. You told me so. As I said, give you half a chance and you'll turn into the kind of woman who spends the day cleaning and baking apple pies and sewing frills—who worries more about dirt on the carpet than she does about her unfortunate husband who, when he comes home tired from work, is treated to an endless litany of domestic trivia—and complaints because he's not earning enough money for new slip-covers or new cushions, or wallpaper in the latest fashionable shade. Whatever happens to be the whine of the week——'

'Clayte,' said Georgina, interrupting him quite gently, because she could tell from his voice that he was referring to some episode from his past that he had learned to deal with in his own way, but which had left him with an acid contempt for all things pertaining to domesticity, 'Clayte, were you married once? That's why you're so adamant, isn't it? You're talking about your wife.'

Clayte swung the wheel to the right and swerved around a corner with a very faint squeal of brakes. 'No,' he said. 'I've made plenty of mistakes in my time, but marriage is not, and never will be, one of them. I have not, and never will have, a wife.' He laughed unpleasantly. 'So, my dear, you can wipe that sweetly sympathetic look off your face and go back to worrying about what colour soap would look best in your bathroom.'

CHAPTER FIVE

GEORGINA gasped. As far as she was concerned, Clayte's sneering attack was totally unprovoked. But there seemed to be a deep core of bitterness in her unpredictable boss that she didn't—and probably didn't want to—understand. There was nothing she could do about it anyway. But she could do something to protect herself from barbs she had done nothing to deserve. One thing Gordon's desertion had taught her was that she was strong enough in herself never to bleed for any man again.

'Clayte,' she said, very clearly and coldly, 'I don't know what, or who, has turned you into the kind of man you are, but I *do* know that I don't have to put up with your insults. I have nothing to apologise for. And if this is your idea of making amends for your *occasional* lapses——'

'It isn't,' he said shortly.

'No? In that case an apology will do nicely.'

For a few seconds a silence broken only by the sound of the engine seemed to electrify the interior of the car. Then, to Georgina's astonishment, Clayte gave a snort that sounded suspiciously like a laugh. 'Do you know who you remind me of?' he asked.

'No. Should I?'

He shrugged. 'I suppose not. But in some ways you're a lot like my aunt Josephine. She never let me get away with much either. All right, Mrs Kettrick, I apologise for even hinting that you might be a soap-obsessed bore.'

'Is that the best you can do?' Georgina was amazed to find that instead of wanting to hit him she was actually biting back a laugh. 'Because if it is, that's just about the worst apology I've ever heard.'

Clayte took his eyes from the road and said quite seriously, 'I expect it is. I don't usually make them.'

'I didn't think you did,' said Georgina drily.

He took one hand off the wheel and patted her absently on the thigh. 'I didn't mean...' He stopped abruptly as something vital and urgent sparked between them. Their eyes met, and in that instant both of them knew that if he should pull the car to the side of the road in the next few minutes they would go no further this evening.

'Tell me—tell me about your aunt Josephine,' gulped Georgina, dropping her gaze to the hands she was gripping tightly in her lap.

She heard Clayte draw in his breath. 'She was my unofficial aunt,' he said briefly.

'Oh. You mean a family friend?'

'No. My father's second wife. Except he never married her. I used to go and stay with them on holidays.'

The tone of his voice caused Georgina to look up hastily. She did a quick double take. Surely she had to be seeing things. But no. Watching the rugged planes of his profile, she was astounded to note that his features were beginning to relax. A few seconds later his lips parted in an amused, reminiscent sort of smile.

'Did you like your aunt Josephine?' she asked doubtfully.

'Very much.'

'Oh. And your mother—was she reconciled——?'

'My mother,' he said drily, 'had her house. And she had me, which I'm not sure she considered much of a

blessing.' His lips twisted. 'I guess I can't blame her for
that.'

Neither could Georgina. Blessing was not a word she
would have used in connection with Clayte.

'No,' she agreed, remembering what had started this
conversation. 'Nor can you hold it against all
womankind because some of us happen to enjoy looking
after a house.'

'I can hold anything against anyone I choose.' He
slowed the car and turned towards her, stretching an arm
along the back of the seat. 'I don't know what gives you
the idea, though, that I have anything at all against
womankind. Quite the contrary. Except, of course, for
the ones who bake me apple pies.'

The words seemed casual, arrogant even, but she didn't
miss the underlying warning. And, as so often happened
around Clayte, Georgina felt her temper rising. 'You
don't really believe the entire female population of the
world is just panting to bake you pies, I hope?' she said
tartly.

'Not at all. I've known the odd one who's threatened
to blend me into a purée and use me in the filling,
though.' He lifted a finger and flipped a short curl on
her neck.

'I know the feeling,' muttered Georgina. But her burst
of temper subsided as quickly as it had arisen.

'Hmm.' Clayte eyed her thoughtfully, then turned his
eyes back to the road. 'You, my girl, had better learn
to be careful.'

'Careful of what?' she scoffed.

'Me,' he replied, without elaborating.

Georgina studied the aggressive set of his jaw, and the
hard light in the one eye she could see, and decided not
to press the matter further. Clayte's hands were safely

on the wheel now, but there was no reason to assume they would stay there.

Twenty minutes later they arrived at the Canadian border. Three-quarters of an hour after that they reached the head of a long line of vehicles, and managed to convince a bored Customs officer that they weren't carrying drugs, alcohol or guns. Finally they crossed the line into Canada.

'Where are you taking me?' asked Georgina, struck by a sudden, unaccountable alarm. She wasn't sure why her nerves had all at once kicked into high gear at the thought of 'doing the town' with Clayte, of perhaps having to dance with him again. But they had. Maybe it was because the dangerous excitement of being held in his powerful arms had once before overwhelmed her with panic. It wasn't that she didn't trust him exactly, but she was beginning to wonder if she trusted herself. Also they were a long way from home.

'Where would you like me to take you?' he asked.

'Somewhere peaceful. I'm not in the mood for crowds and noise,' she told him firmly.

'Are you ever?' That dry, faintly mocking tone again.

'Yes,' she snapped. 'I'm not a total hermit, Clayte. I like people. But it's been a long day and I'm tired.'

Clayte nodded. 'OK, you've made your point.'

He didn't say anything further until he turned the car off a long street lined with neat houses, and began to drive past a sweeping expanse of darkness that Georgina supposed must be grass. Then they were circling upwards through the shadowy shapes of trees until they came to the top of a small hill crowned by a dome-shaped glass bubble. It reflected the soft light of the early moon like some unexpected vision of outer space.

Clayte pulled to a stop at the edge of the road and climbed out to open her door. 'Where are we?' she asked, puzzled, as he took her arm and led her past the bubble to a low wall overlooking the city.

'Little Mountain. This is Queen Elizabeth Park. I hope it's peaceful enough for you.' He gestured at the lights of Vancouver spreading into the distance below them, a brilliant kaleidoscope of gold patterned against the dark backdrop of the night. In the distance, fairy ski-lights betrayed the invisible presence of Grouse Mountain.

There were people moving in the shadows beside them, mostly couples like themselves. But Clayte was right. It was a peaceful place to soak up the fragrance of the night. She could smell the sweet scent of flowers on the air.

Georgina took a deep breath, savouring the calm and tranquillity. A soft breeze lifted her hair, and when she turned to Clayte she was smiling.

'It's lovely,' she said simply.

He was watching the curls dance across her forehead, and to her bewilderment he frowned suddenly, as though smitten by an unexpected pain.

'Yes,' he replied. 'It is. So are you.' He shoved his hands into his pockets and glared down at her almost as if he regretted having spoken. But when she turned away, confused, he muttered something under his breath and dropped an arm lightly across her shoulder. It was a careless enough gesture, intended to make up for his ill-humour, Georgina supposed. And his arm felt right there. Comfortable. She had to force herself to remember who he was, knowing that if she allowed herself to forget it would be all too easy to let her body lean back into his—to lift up her face to be kissed . . . because he had called her lovely . . .

'They used to quarry for stone here. I'd show you the quarry gardens, but it's dark,' Clayte interrupted her reverie abruptly. She wondered if he had read her thoughts and was nipping them off at the pass. She turned away to look at the lights.

They stood there for some time, watching the branches of the trees stir softly, and absorbing the quiet beauty of the night. Then Georgina became aware that Clayte had taken her hand, and that his thumb was gently stroking her palm. She felt an immediate arousal deep inside. It frightened her—and excited her—and at once she tried to pull away.

Clayte didn't let go. 'What's the matter?' he asked. 'Afraid the magic of the night will overcome me, tempt me to sling you across my saddle and ride off into the stars? Don't worry, I'm not very susceptible to magic.'

'Nor do you have a saddle,' she reminded him, trying not to let images of magic and stars destroy her precarious control. 'Clayte, what's in that incredible glass bubble?' Just at this moment she didn't much care what was in the bubble, but she hoped it would steer his mind in a more prosaic direction.

It did. 'That's the Bloedel Conservatory,' he replied in a brisk, tour-guide voice—almost as if he had never heard of magic. 'It's a tropical garden and aviary. But I'm afraid it's closed now. So you'll have to find something else to distract me.'

'Do you need distracting?'

When Clayte smiled his slow, lazy smile at her and said that he rather thought he did, she immediately wished she hadn't asked. She tugged at her imprisoned hand with a kind of desperation, and this time he let it go at once.

They walked back to the car a few minutes later, and Georgina made sure there was a space of several feet between them—which, to her chagrin, appeared to afford Clayte great amusement.

'It's getting late,' she said decisively, as they fastened their seatbelts. 'I think we ought to go home.'

'Nonsense,' replied Clayte. 'You can't tell me a long drive, Canada Customs and a view from the top of a hill is your idea of an evening's fun and frolic.'

'No, but I didn't want to frolic in the first place. I'm not a gazelle. And *you* may be on holiday, but I have a job to go to in the morning. A job at *your* hotel.'

'I'm not on holiday, you know. As a matter of fact, I'm checking up on you.' He gave her a bland smile that made her want to hit him.

So that was what had brought him back so quickly. He didn't trust her to run the Inn without his supervision. She bit her lip, and stared grimly out of the window. It looked as though her job would be short-lived.

'Now what's the matter?' he asked with a touch of impatience, as he steered the car swiftly down the hill and into traffic.

'Just that you don't seem to have any faith in my ability. Did you check up on Steve Novak a week after *he* took over at the Inn?' She folded a pleat in her linen skirt, and it left a crease.

Clayte made a sound that she supposed was his way of expressing derision—a cross between a snort and a laugh. 'No. That's precisely why I'm checking up on you.'

'Oh. You mean it's not just because I'm a—a woman?'

To her surprise, he didn't answer at once. Instead he swung the car round a corner and came to a stop in front of a sign that read 'Pooch and Pig Inn'.

'Why are we stopping?' asked Georgina suspiciously, as he came round to open her door.

'Because I'm thinking of buying this place and I'd like to observe its operation incognito.' He held out his hand to help her out.

'What you mean is that you'd like to avoid answering my question.'

'No, what I mean is that a few minutes looking at a view isn't my idea of an evening on the town. But since you're resolutely opposed to such levity I may as well accomplish a bit of business.' When Georgina didn't move he took hold of her wrist and ordered, 'Out. Stop looking at me as though you suspect me of white slavery.'

A young couple passed by them arm in arm. They stared curiously at the tall, arresting man and the pretty woman who was glaring up at him as if she'd like to stamp on his feet. Georgina saw the curious glances and realised they were attracting attention. And Clayte still had hold of her wrist.

'Very well,' she said coldly. 'If you must employ caveman tactics.'

'I am not employing caveman tactics. Cavemen grab their women by the hair when the need arises. Which, come to think of it, might not be such a bad idea.' He ran his free hand slowly through her wind-blown curls and she shivered suddenly.

Georgina gave up, not because she was intimidated, but because she was genuinely tired and it seemed the sanest course of action. Maybe if she did as he wanted he would get her home some time before sunrise. She rose with as much dignity as she could gather round her and stalked ahead of him into the Pooch and Pig Inn.

The lobby was not unlike the one at Snowlake, and Georgina could see why it had caught Clayte's interest—especially when he turned to her and said brusquely, 'You'll be relieved to hear you don't have to dance. No dance-floor. Which isn't much of a problem, as the Willow Inns' clientele don't generally go in for riotous nightlife.'

'Neither do I,' said Georgina.

'So I've observed.' He spoke with such grim reticence that she wasn't surprised when he took her by the arm, escorted her to the darkest corner of the lounge, and added coolly, 'Perhaps this will suit your modest and retiring sensibilities.'

Now what have I done? wondered Georgina as she glanced round the intimate little pub. The tables were lit by red candles in old-fashioned brass candle-holders, and she was glad to sink into the shadows where every unwary expression wouldn't run the risk of giving away her thoughts—which at the moment were engaged in delightfully unladylike fantasies of punching Clayte O'Neill's supercilious nose.

'Now, what was your question?' he asked calmly, after giving their orders to the bartender and settling himself back in his chair.

'I asked,' said Georgina, regretfully swallowing the fantasies, 'whether you felt I needed more supervision than Steve Novak because I'm a woman.'

'Could be,' he said, laconic now as he leaned back further and rested an ankle on his knee. 'I've asked the same question of myself. I like supervising you, Georgina.'

'Well, I don't like being supervised,' she snapped. 'Unless it's necessary. Which it hasn't been.'

'Mmm. I've noticed you don't take direction very well.'

The bartender came with Clayte's beer and her white wine, and it was several seconds before Georgina was able to unclench her teeth and reply with apparent composure, 'Clayte, I don't need directing. I know what I'm doing. And if something does come up that I can't cope with, or that I think you should know about, I'll let you know.'

'OK, Mrs Kettrick. I'll buy that. And I apologise for treating you as a woman.' She could just make out his provocative smile in the dim lighting. 'I guess it must have been all that knitting and cooking that did it. By the way, did I tell you that beige suit of yours is quite attractive?'

He was baiting her. She wasn't sure why, except that it seemed to be a habit of his. Indeed he often seemed to go out of his way to annoy her. But she had him this time.

'Yes, you did. I made it,' she said smugly. 'On my sewing machine.'

It wasn't so dark in the pub that she couldn't see his black eyes narrow. But, to her surprise, instead of making some defensive or scathing retort, he picked up his glass, leaned his head against the wall and exclaimed, 'Well, I'll be damned! Nice one, Georgina. Well done.'

He was laughing at her again, and yet somehow she knew he meant it. He didn't in the least mind her one-upping him. He delighted in aggravating her because that seemed to be the way he was made. But when she got the better of him he was more than willing to acknowledge her victory.

She liked him for that, but as she didn't particularly want to like him it didn't help much. Liking could too easily turn into something else, and she had no intention of losing her heart to a man who would love her, perhaps, and then leave her the moment he caught sight of an apple pie. When, and if, she loved again, her heart would go to someone who wanted the same things she wanted. Roots and a home and a family. If she never met that someone—well, at least she was well satisfied with her job.

If she managed to keep that job. Which, thanks to the unpredictable man sitting across from her, was by no means certain.

Clayte disappeared a few minutes later, and she supposed he was busy being incognito. By the time he returned, Georgina had already finished her drink. This time when she asked to be taken home he made no objection.

She fell asleep in the car on the way back, and was hardly aware of passing through American Customs. In fact she wasn't aware of anything much until cool air hit her face and she opened her eyes to find herself suspended several feet above the ground. One of Clayte's arms was around her shoulders, the other beneath her knees, and he was carrying her up the path to her cottage.

'Wh-what?' she gasped as he reached the step. 'What are you doing . . . ?'

He bent his head. 'Nothing, at the moment. Just making sure my manager doesn't fall asleep on her doorstep. Why? Is there something you'd like me to do?'

As the heat of his body began to permeate her skin, and she found her gaze riveted on the sensual fullness of his lips, she realised there was very definitely something she would like him to do. But no way in the world would she admit it, even though she suspected he knew.

'No,' she said. 'No, nothing. I——'

'I thought not.' He stared down at her for a moment with an ironic little glint in his eye, then tipped her upright. 'OK, where's your key?'

'Under that flowerpot.'

'That's a damn fool place to put it. Anyone could walk in.'

'I suppose so, but I'm always changing purses. And this is Snowlake.'

'Snowlake,' he said roughly, 'is no more immune to crime than anywhere else.' He lifted the pot, found the key and fitted it into the lock. Then he put both hands round her waist, opened the door with his foot and pushed her firmly inside.

For an endless moment, Georgina held her breath. But this time it wasn't his touch that made her heart stop. She groaned softly. No! Please. It couldn't be—she must be hallucinating. She rubbed her eyes, looked again. Surely it wasn't possible. This couldn't be her own beloved home...

But of course it could.

'Oh, my God,' she cried, turning to Clayte and flinging her arms round his neck without pausing to think what she was doing. 'Oh, Clayte. You were right. Look. Look what's happened. Somebody—somebody *has* broken in.'

'So I see.' Clayte's voice was clipped, furious, as he disengaged her arms and deposited her in the daisy-patterned chair. 'OK, take it easy. You sit tight while I make sure they've actually gone. Then we'll call the police.'

Georgina sat tight, huddled into the chair and staring with mindless disbelief at the incredible disorder the thieves had made of her neatly ordered room. The room she had taken such pride in.

Her small television set and radio had gone. So had her stereo, leaving gaping, empty spaces against the wall. Her beloved chiming mantel-clock was missing too. A tumbled pile of Delft figurines lay in its place. The thieves had left those, along with her Royal Worcester plates. But she could see that the silver wine goblets her aunt had given her and Gordon as a wedding present were gone. And a jumble of compact discs were scattered all over the sofa. Presumably the thieves didn't share her classical tastes. They'd taken her crystal vase, though, and thrown its bunch of yellow roses on to the floor.

She closed her eyes.

'Long gone, obviously.' Clayte's harsh voice broke into her thoughts. 'They even put the key back where they found it. Thoughtful of them.' He picked up the phone and began to dial with angry, abrupt movements. A few minutes later, after reporting the break-in succinctly and with a minimum of verbiage, he put down the receiver with a crash.

Georgina stared up at him wordlessly as he stood with his hands in his pockets surveying the devastation. His jaw was thrust upwards and his eyes were as hard as black diamonds.

'Not much damage,' he rapped out after a moment. 'Just an incredible mess. Your thieves weren't malicious, Georgina, which is more of a break than you deserve. Anyone stupid enough to leave a key under a flower-pot——' He broke off when he caught sight of her face. 'Never mind, it's too late for that, isn't it?' His dark brows drew together as he went on grimly, 'Your bedroom drawers have all been emptied on to the floor, but I can't see that anything's broken. You'd better check it. The police will want to know if anything's missing.'

'Yes.' Georgina tried to stand up, and found that her legs didn't seem to want to support her. When she looked up at Clayte with desperation in her eyes, she thought for a moment that she saw an unusual softening of his features. But almost at once he became brisk and authoritarian again.

'Come on,' he said, moving to her side and putting both hands underneath her arms. 'I know it's been a shock, but the best way to handle it is to deal with it.'

She nodded, seeming to have lost the power of speech, and allowed him to pull her to her feet and put his arm around her to support her into the small, cosy haven of her bedroom. At least it *had* been a haven before tonight. Now, as Clayte had warned her, every drawer had been up-ended on to the floor, and although the blue and white curtains and the blue check bedspread had not been touched it seemed as if they'd been sullied in some way. The room was her refuge no longer. It belonged to strangers. Unclean strangers. Vaguely, she remembered the teenager who had watched her take the key from under the flowerpot. How could she have been such a fool...?

She looked up at Clayte, stricken, and his arm tightened a fraction.

'Did you keep any valuables in here?' he demanded, forcing her to face up to reality.

She shook her head. 'No. All my money was in my purse. And I didn't have any good jewellery except for the gold earrings I'm wearing. I—I could never afford it.'

Again she thought she saw that unexpected softness in his eyes, but all he said was, 'Better take a look anyway.'

She did, and as she searched through the rubble of her possessions the unnatural numbness that had dulled her feelings at first began to turn into a slow, burning anger. How dared those avaricious thugs break into her home, steal her property and create havoc in every room they touched? She felt violated, furious, wanting to strike back but unable to connect with the right target. She thought Clayte understood, because she read something of the sort on his face too.

The police came then, took statements from both of them, and checked the house for evidence and prints. They also told Georgina not to leave keys under flower-pots, and got her to make a list of missing items. When she asked if there was much chance of having her be-longings returned, they shrugged and said there was always that possibility; they would do their best.

After they left, Clayte helped her to tidy up the mess and then, to her stupefaction, pushed her firmly down on to the sofa and told her he was going to make tea.

'But you can't,' she said. 'You don't know how.'

He smiled cynically. 'I know a lot more than you think. Put your feet up.'

When she only gaped at him, he strode back to her side, swung her legs on to the sofa and removed her shoes. 'I'll be back in a minute,' he said tersely. 'Don't move.'

Georgina didn't want to move. She was still consumed with anger. The knowledge that her secure home was no longer secure—and never had been—was hard to bear. But she was also desperately weary. If she tried to stand up she was almost sure her legs would fold up like rubber bands.

Clayte came back carrying two cups containing a liquid which, to her vague surprise, actually tasted like tea.

'Right,' he said, settling himself in the pink-flowered armchair and looking a bit like a Venus flytrap among the daisies, 'drink that up, and then off you go to bed.'

'I can't—I don't want...' Her voice trailed off. How could she tell him that she was afraid to go to bed? Rationally, she knew there was no chance that the thieves would come back. They already had all they wanted. Unfortunately, there was nothing rational about her feeling of insecurity and violation, as if her privacy had been permanently invaded.

'You don't want to be alone,' Clayte finished for her. 'Naturally I've no intention of leaving. You'll be quite safe.'

'But I...' She swallowed. Didn't he know that with him in the house she'd feel safe in one sense, but dangerously at risk in another?

Apparently he did. 'I'll sleep on the sofa,' he said gruffly. 'I wasn't planning on adding insult to injury.'

He looked angry. Had her thoughts been as transparent as that? 'Thank you,' she murmured. 'I—are you sure you don't mind?'

'Mind sleeping on that apology for a flowerbed? Sure I mind. But I don't see any alternative, do you?'

'Well, I—no, I suppose not.'

He sighed. 'Georgina, I'm not Bluebeard, but I am a man. I'm just as aware as you are of the temptations inherent in sharing your bed. So I'll take the sofa.'

She nodded, feeling foolish although she wasn't quite sure why. 'All right. I—I appreciate it. It's very nice of you.'

'I am never nice,' said Clayte bitingly. 'I do, however, have a healthy interest in the welfare of my managers. Have you finished that tea?'

'Yes.'

'Good. Then go to bed.'

Georgina stood up, feeling even more foolish when she stumbled over her feet on the way to the hall. As she closed the door carefully behind her, she had a feeling that Clayte's eyes were boring into her back.

She was already lying in bed in her chaste white cotton nightgown when it occurred to her that she hadn't even offered him a blanket. She groaned, and reached for her robe.

At the door of the living-room she hesitated. 'Clayte?' she murmured half-heartedly. 'Are you awake?'

'Very much so.' His grim voice reached her loud and clear.

'Oh. Are you cold? Do you need a blanket?'

'Believe me, it's not lack of heat that's keeping me awake. Go back to bed, Georgina.'

'But I——'

Abruptly the door was flung open. 'For heaven's sake, woman, don't you have the self-preservative instincts of a flea? Do you actually want me to join you in that virginal bed?'

Georgina stepped back, gaping. He was wearing only brief black undershorts, and just for a moment she had a crazy urge to answer, Yes, please. But if she did that her instincts, which were considerably more useful than a flea's, told her she might regret it till her dying day. There was also a good chance she'd lose her job. Clayte wasn't the kind of man who believed in having affairs with his staff, and if anyone came out the loser in an encounter of that sort it was a safe bet it wouldn't be him.

She stared at the bronzed flesh so tantalisingly exposed and wondered if he knew what he was asking. 'No,' she replied, with an almost audible sigh. 'I don't want you to join me. Goodnight, Clayte.'

She turned away, and it wasn't until she was back in her bed that his choice of words finally sank in. He had called her bed 'virginal'. She ran the back of her hand across her forehead. Well, it might as well be the truth, mightn't it? And it hadn't bothered her much for a long time. But it was certainly bothering her now.

Just at this moment she wasn't sure what disturbed her more—the robbery, or Clayte's virile presence in the next room. She was still trying to resolve the issue when she fell asleep.

'Georgina. Wake up.'

Georgina blinked. Where was she? She couldn't be in the cottage because . . . Oh. Yes, she could. All at once the events of last night washed over her in a horrifying wave. She struggled to sit up, then realised she was wearing her nightgown, and pulled the sheet up to her neck instead.

'That's the idea,' Clayte's voice mocked her. 'Man the barricades.'

Her eyes snapped open. 'You—you shouldn't be in here.'

'Why not? I promise you I can't see a thing. And I've brought you some tea.'

He was standing beside her bed looking delectable in trousers and a shirt he hadn't troubled to button, waving a cup from which the steam rose invitingly. She breathed in the welcome aroma. For a man who loathed all things domestic, Clayte wasn't at all bad at making tea. She wondered if he had other accomplishments hidden up his sleeve.

If he had, they weren't in the culinary line. She discovered that a moment later, when he added, 'Hurry up and drink it. I'm ready for breakfast.'

'Oh. You want me to cook for you?' She didn't quite believe it after all his taunts about pies.

'I want breakfast, if that's what you mean.'

'And I suppose you're not about to make it yourself.'

'Not if I can help it. I'd prefer something more substantial than toast.'

Georgina felt a small glow of superiority. 'Is that all you can manage?' she asked, trying not to let her complacence show.

'Do you want me to prove it to you?'

'No,' she said quickly, not trusting the threat in his eye. The mess she'd cleaned up last night had been bad enough. She wasn't interested in having her kitchen turned into a test site. 'Go away, and I'll come and cook you something as soon as I'm dressed.'

Clayte departed wearing a small, smug smile.

It wasn't until Georgina entered the living-room, decently dressed in her suit, that last night's desecration hit her like a bomb. The cottage was tidy enough now, but her missing clock and television left glaring spaces, reminding her that her peaceful seclusion, her much loved home, were not inviolate. Security was a very ephemeral thing. She wondered if she would ever feel totally safe here again.

When she went into the kitchen, Clayte was standing in front of an open fridge frowning at its neatly ordered contents. Georgina paused. There was something reassuring about that tough, masculine back that seemed a little too large for the small room. Suddenly she didn't feel quite so vulnerable any more.

'Don't stand there window-shopping,' she said automatically. 'You're letting all the cold out.'

Clayte closed the door and turned round. He had buttoned his shirt now, but the expression on his face made her flinch. It was a mixture of disbelief and disgust, as if he had just seen a particularly repulsive ghost who was asking him to clean the drains.

'What's the matter?' she demanded, not understanding what she'd done.

'Nothing much.' His voice grated like sandpaper. 'Your choice of words, those carefully organised shelves—they reminded me of your housewifely prowess.'

'I presume that's not a compliment,' said Georgina, wondering at his unwarranted harshness, and wondering also why it hurt so much.

'You presume right.' He sat down at the table and crossed his arms. 'What's for breakfast?'

'Oh, so you've no objection to my taking on the housewifely task of making breakfast,' she said tartly. 'What a relief.'

'Don't be impertinent,' he growled. 'I'm still your boss, remember.'

Yes, she supposed he was, for as long as she chose to put up with him and his job. And he *had* been concerned enough about her to stay the night—without even attempting to take advantage of the volatile situation. Perhaps it wasn't altogether surprising that he was in a bad mood. He couldn't have spent a very comfortable night trying to compress his large frame on to her sofa.

'What would you like for breakfast?' she asked coolly. She supposed she owed him that much in return for his help.

'Eggs. Bacon. Plenty of toast. And more tea.'

Just as if he's giving orders in a restaurant, thought Georgina. 'Yes, sir,' she said woodenly. 'Coming right up.'

He nodded, apparently unaware of her sarcasm, and picked up the morning paper. Scowling but efficient, Georgina went about the task of preparing breakfast. Clayte ate it with no sign of appreciation and no conversation as he continued to study the paper from front to back.

My paper, thought Georgina resentfully. Usually she read it with *her* breakfast. Today all she had to look at was the top of Clayte's head and an advertisement for a hair restorant. When the plates were empty she stood up, and something—the position of the sun in the blue sky perhaps—made her look at her watch. She hadn't thought of the time until this moment. Her mind had been too full of other things.

She gasped. 'Clayte! Do you realise it's after ten? The Inn——'

He looked up with a slight frown between his eyebrows and said dismissively, 'I have informed the staff that you won't be in today. Later on I'll check things over myself.'

'But you'd no right. You can't——'

'I have every right. The Willow Inn happens to belong to me. And I can. I have.'

'But why? I'm perfectly capable——'

'I'm sure you are. However, you had one hell of a shock last night, and you'll find you have a lot to see to today. Insurance for one thing. I suppose you *do* have insurance?'

'I'm not a complete nitwit, Clayte O'Neill.'

'If you were, you can bet your boots you wouldn't be working for me.' Clayte turned back to the paper, and Georgina had a feeling he resented her presence even though this was her home and not his. Biting her lip, she went on clearing the table.

What a delightfully old-fashioned scene, she thought bitterly, as she loaded clean dishes in the rack. Straight out of Dickens. Husband reading paper and stuffing his face, while little woman scurries around waiting on him and doing all the chores.

She stopped scurrying abruptly, and let her arms drop to her sides. *What* had she just called him? Husband? Clayte? That was a laugh! Clayte, who had assured her he would never be any woman's husband, who had spent his life avoiding even the remotest hint of a matrimonial coil.

She stole a quick look at him over her shoulder, and noted the dark hair waving seductively on his neck. Husband indeed. Yes, that was a laugh all right. She went on doing the dishes, and wondered vaguely why she wasn't actually laughing.

Fifteen minutes later Clayte laid down the paper and stood up. 'Will you be all right?' he asked abruptly.

'Of course. Why shouldn't I be?'

'Not nervous?'

Georgina shrugged. 'I can't spend the rest of my life jumping at shadows just because my house was broken into.'

'No, you can't. OK, I'll see you later.'

She swallowed. 'Why? Aren't you going back to Los Angeles?'

'I hadn't thought of it. Anxious to see the back of me, are you? I wonder now, what *does* go on behind my hotel's antique doors? Am I missing something?' He was looking at her with that bold challenge in his eye again, and she knew he had conquered his earlier ill-humour. She turned away quickly so that he wouldn't see her blush.

'Nothing goes on,' she said, shoving a stack of plates on to a shelf. 'And you're not missing anything.'

'How very dull.'

Before she could think of a suitably deflating response, he had thrown his jacket over his shoulder and was already striding down the path.

'Make the most of your day off,' he called back to her. 'You won't get another free one for a while. I'll see you this evening.'

Oh, will you? thought Georgina, as the car door slammed. Don't I even have a say in the matter?

When she sat down by the phone to call her insurance company, though, it came to her that probably she had no say at all. Clayte made the rules, and his staff observed them, even when they weren't officially on duty.

She spent the rest of the day dealing with insurance and cleaning her house from top to bottom—not only because it needed it after the activities of the burglars and the police, but because she couldn't feel clean again, couldn't feel the cottage was her own, until she had scrubbed away all evidence of the break-in.

At about four o'clock, just as she was brewing herself a well-deserved pot of tea, her doorbell pealed. When she didn't answer at once, it rang three more times in rapid succession.

'What's the emergency?' she demanded, flinging the door open, and not in much doubt about whom she would find on the step.

'I have a plane to catch,' Clayte replied shortly. He moved her aside and stepped in without being asked. 'Before I go, there's some work to be done around here.'

Georgina gaped at him. 'Plane?' she repeated, latching on to the only word that got through to her. 'But I thought you said you weren't leaving.'

'I wasn't. Something's come up in San Diego. A business deal I've been working on for months.'

'Oh.' She winced as he emptied a bag full of hardware all over her freshly polished coffee-table. 'Then what are you doing here?'

'Making this place a lot more burglar-proof.' He pulled off his dark jacket and flung it over a chair. 'I don't want you living in this fishbowl without so much as a deadbolt lock or a peephole between you and Snowlake's criminal element.'

'Peephole?' said Georgina blankly. She felt curiously blank all over. 'Why a peephole?'

'So you can check out your visitors before you open the door to further trouble.'

As Georgina watched, mouth agape, he strode past her and started doing something with a brace and bit.

'You're making a hole in the wood,' she protested.

'That's the general idea.' He continued to make swift, efficient movements with his muscular forearms, and she watched him as if she'd turned to stone. She felt like stone. Numb all over, and she couldn't understand why.

Clayte finished installing the peephole and immediately started on the locks. But still Georgina couldn't find her voice. He wasn't saying much either. Nor was he wasting any time.

'When does your plane leave?' she managed finally, when, without looking at her or asking her permission, he began to screw clamps on to the windows.

'In an hour.' He gave a last vigorous twist, laid his tools back on the table, and straightened slowly.

Georgina nodded, moistened lips that had gone uncomfortably dry, and said, 'You haven't much time, then.'

'No.' He shrugged on his jacket, his dark features unusually sober. 'Georgina, are you sure you're all right? Because if you're going to see gremlins in every shadow I'll get Agnes——'

'I don't need a babysitter, Clayte. I'm used to being alone.'

Funny, but it was true. Her panic of last night had subsided, and she was no longer afraid that the burglars would return. But, inexplicably, she found that she didn't at all want Clayte to go.

He lifted his shoulders. 'OK. I believe you. Let me know if you have any problems.'

'You mean at the Inn?'

Something that was probably irritation sparked very briefly in his eyes. 'I mean anywhere.'

Georgina frowned. That didn't make sense. 'Thank you,' she said doubtfully. 'It's very kind——'

'It's not very kind,' he interrupted harshly. 'It's intelligent self-interest.'

'If you say so.' There wasn't much point in arguing. If Clayte said his concern for her was motivated purely by self-interest—well, he ought to know. Somehow the thought didn't do much to cheer her.

He was standing by the door now, his hard eyes fixed on her face. Then slowly, as she stared back at him, he let his gaze move down over her bright red T-shirt and smoothly fitting jeans, then back up again. 'Very nice,' he said dispassionately. 'Those jeans look good on you.'

'Sure they do.' She answered him with a bitterness that surprised her. 'I'm just your average country girl, Mr O'Neill. Slinky, sophisticated silk never did do much for me.' She held out her hand. 'Thank you for everything. I am grateful.'

'How grateful?'

A small, provocative smile played at the corners of his mouth, and Georgina was fairly sure she took his meaning. But he was only baiting her. He didn't mean a word of it, and he expected her to back away, to play the shrinking violet to his Bluebeard. It had always amused him to mock her...

This time the spark was in Georgina's eye as some devil that was two parts indignation and one part pure physical frustration made her move towards him, swivelling her hips in the tight jeans.

'Very grateful,' she purred, as she saw his nostrils flare. 'Would you like me to show you how grateful?'

When her breasts were almost touching his chest, she lifted her arms and placed them around his neck.

CHAPTER SIX

GEORGINA stared into Clayte's eyes, saw inky darkness starkly contrasting with white. She watched the heavy lids droop. And then she felt his hands close over her hips, move slowly down to circle her thighs. She gave a small gasp as a shock of desire flamed up and exploded unbearably, so that it was all she could do not to cry out. Clayte splayed his fingers, and she lifted her lips for his kiss.

It didn't come. Inexplicably, unbelievably, he was holding her away.

'And what the hell, Mrs Kettrick,' he asked conversationally, 'do you happen to think you were doing?'

Georgina hadn't suffered the pain of a divorce, and the break-up of countless budding friendships through her parents' often precipitate moves, without learning how to hide her hurts. She was disorientated, embarrassed, furious with Clayte for his part in this idiotic drama, but she wasn't about to let go of her pride.

'Being grateful,' she replied, folding her hands demurely in front of her. 'Wasn't that what you wanted?'

His lips, those lips that had not touched hers, twisted cynically. 'What I want, Mrs K, and what I expected to get are two different matters entirely.'

'And what did you expect to get?' asked Georgina, summoning an innocent smile.

He sent her a repressive look that ought to have reduced her to jelly but somehow didn't. 'I'm not at all sure, but keep it up and I promise you, you needn't have any doubts about what *you'll* get.'

Georgina gave an affected little shiver. 'Ooh, Mr O'Neill,' she giggled, 'you do terrify me. I never thought you'd turn out to be the violent type.'

Clayte compressed his lips and took a step towards her. When she backed away, still giggling, he reached for her arm. Her eyes widened, and abruptly he came to a halt. All of a sudden he didn't look threatening any more, he looked tired, and when she murmured a doubtful, 'Clayte?' he passed a hand over his eyes and stood for a minute with his head bent, not speaking.

Then he looked up and said heavily, 'Let's stop playing games, shall we, Georgina?'

'Games?' she repeated warily.

'That's what I said. The truth of the matter is that we'd both like to take our relationship one step further——'

'I wouldn't,' said Georgina. 'I'm not interested in a relationship, Clayte.'

'I know. For you it's permanence, picket fences and roses, or nothing at all. For me, quite simply, it's the opposite. Freedom from precisely those restraints. I'd break down your picket fence if I didn't suspect you'd retaliate by baking me pies. Or even . . .' He shuddered. 'Or maybe even knitting me a sweater.'

'No, Clayte,' said Georgina, refusing to respond to gibes behind which she sensed something far deeper than his natural tendency to mock. 'I won't let you break down my fence.'

'And, more importantly, I won't even try.' He looked at his watch, as if the conversation was beginning to bore him. 'My time's run out, I'm afraid. Goodbye, Georgina. Do you suppose we can safely shake hands?'

She stared at his outstretched palm and then, reluctantly, placed her small hand in his. His fingers curled around it, and she saw a look she couldn't interpret in his eyes. For just a moment she wondered if he was as confused as she was, but almost at once he smiled, a wry, unconsciously seductive smile, and said lightly, 'Goodbye, Mrs Kettrick. I don't anticipate further problems at the Inn, but do try to keep a lid on Alexander.'

Georgina nodded, once more speechless, and Clayte turned away. She closed her eyes, waiting for the sound of the door closing. But she heard nothing. Then she started as firm fingers tilted up her chin, and she felt the soft, feather-light pressure of a man's lips touching her forehead. Next they were on her nose, and after that, for less than a second, and so softly that she wasn't sure it had actually happened, on her mouth.

She opened her eyes. Clayte was already at the door. He didn't look back.

'What is it, Jill?' Georgina looked up from the budget printouts she was studying, some sixth sense telling her that her new assistant hadn't come into the office merely to deliver letters for signing.

'We're overbooked,' said Jill, as if she were announcing the crack of doom. 'The couple in Room 14 won't leave, and Mr Storey's been in a car accident. He's in hospital. Naturally his wife wants to stay on. And there's an advance party from the plumbers' conference in the lobby giving Lori a bad time because their rooms aren't ready.'

'Why aren't they ready?' Georgina was pretty certain she already knew the answer, but it was always as well to be sure.

'All the graphic artists stayed on till the last minute. Housekeeping couldn't finish in time.'

Georgina sighed. It was an old story. Guests who left late, guests who came early, frazzled housekeeping staff doing their best under Agnes's expert supervision. Thank goodness Agnes had finally consented to take the job on a permanent basis. That was the only bright spot in a day that had already been littered with minefields.

She stood up and prepared to begin the process of soothing the plumbers. As she followed Jill out of her office Georgina reflected, not for the first time, that it was odd how her feelings had changed in the past two months. She still loved the challenge of her job, but ever since the day Clayte left Snowlake she had felt that something was missing. The old contentment she had known as head housekeeper was gone. But contentment wasn't what she longed for any more. There seemed to be a sort of emptiness in her life, as if it had lost its foundation. Sometimes she felt exactly as she had as a child when her parents had casually announced that they were moving on again—which meant that she wouldn't be able to take part in the school play, or the camping trip, or go to the concert with a boy who had finally plucked up courage to ask her out.

She had thought those days were over at last, but now it seemed that security and her beloved home were not enough. The break-in had brought home to her that all safe havens were ephemeral—but it wasn't just that...

She shook her head. Jill had turned round to see if she was coming, and she remembered she was supposed to be dealing with plumbers, not pondering the meaning of her life. As for Clayte, she was glad he had maintained his contact with Snowlake entirely through Fred Charlton, his executive assistant, and she wasn't in the least disappointed that he hadn't once reappeared to disrupt her efficient running of the Inn.

She smiled at Jill and hurried into the lobby. Half an hour later the plumbers were suitably soothed, the occupants of Room 14 were packing, happily bribed by the offer of a free night's accommodation elsewhere, and Mrs Storey had been assured she could stay.

Georgina heaved a sigh of relief, and was just about to return to her office when her eye was caught by a swirl of black velvet by the doors. She turned, wondering if her imagination was playing tricks on her. It was still only September—much too early for Hallowe'en. But the vision she saw floating through the doorway was no figment of anyone's imagination. Georgina stared, fascinated, at the full-blown figure of a woman in a voluminous flowing black cape. She was tall and white-haired, with a large nose, and her considerable height was accentuated by a huge black picture hat banded by a scarlet ribbon.

Georgina blinked. Was this the latest fashion for plumbers' wives? Somehow she didn't think so. In any case, it wasn't her affair. The registration of guests was Lori's concern, even if they did come disguised as bats in hats.

She turned away, but was immediately halted by a stentorian female voice bellowing, 'You. Young lady with the curly blonde hair. I think I want to talk to you, if you don't mind.'

Georgina did mind, but as she owned the only curly blonde hair in the lobby she had to respond. 'I'm Georgina Kettrick,' she said politely. 'Can I help you?'

'Ah. Good. Thought you were the one.'

Georgina found herself being inspected from top to toe by a pair of button black eyes.

'Er—the one?' she asked doubtfully. 'I'm the manager, if that's——'

'Yup. That's who I want. New manager my nephew says is an obstinate, house-proud little witch who could do with a damned good...' She stopped, seeming to take in the interested eyes of Jill, Lori and a passing bellboy for the first time. 'Never mind. Nephew of mine could do with the odd boot in the backside himself.'

'Nephew?' said Georgina through dry lips. She was almost sure she knew the nephew in question, but she had to be certain.

'Yup. Clayton. Your boss, my dear.'

Georgina nodded, still dazed. 'Would—would you like to come into my office, Mrs—Miss...?'

'McGuigan. Josephine McGuigan. Never was a Mrs.'

Clayte's aunt Josephine. The one he said she, Georgina, reminded him of?

'Please come this way, Ms McGuigan.' She smiled politely, trying not to betray her astonishment. 'Jill...'

'Would you like me to bring you a cup of tea, Georgi?' Jill was always quick on the uptake, and didn't mind performing the occasional service that wasn't in her job description.

Georgina was about to accept when Clayte's aunt exclaimed disgustedly, 'Tea! What I need, young lady, is a good port.'

'Port for Ms McGuigan, please, Jill,' said Georgina faintly. 'I—I'll have a sherry. A small one.' She didn't want a sherry at three in the afternoon, but neither did she want to appear uncivil to Clayte's magnificently improbable aunt.

A few minutes later she had installed Aunt Josephine in the largest armchair in her office, and was settling herself opposite on a swivel chair. Jill, poker-faced, arrived with the drinks on a silver tray. Georgina refused to meet her eyes. If she did, she knew she would almost certainly burst out laughing.

'Now then,' said Aunt Josephine when Jill had gone, 'let's have a look at you.' She threw her cape over the back of her chair, revealing a flowing black crêpe dress with a scarlet sash.

Georgina said nothing as piercing black eyes took in her modest beige suit and cream blouse.

'Yup. You'll do,' Aunt Josephine nodded.

'Um—thank you,' murmured Georgina. 'Er—do for what?'

'For Clayton, of course. Time that boy settled down. He's thirty-five years old, do you know that?'

Georgina did vaguely, but she didn't see what Clayte's age had to do with her.

She said so.

Aunt Josephine gave a snort. 'Ought to have everything to do with you. Needs a sensible woman who won't stand for any of his nonsense. Thought you sounded right when he started swearing. Been meaning to take a look at you for weeks.'

'Swearing?' said Georgina, wondering if Clayte's aunt was getting senile. 'I don't see——'

'Swearing about you, gal. Seems you wouldn't put up with any of his whip-cracking. He's not used to that, but it's what he needs. Not those party girls he usually takes up with when he decides to fit a woman into his schedule.'

Georgina frowned. Josephine McGuigan might think Clayte needed someone like her, but from the sounds of it her hopes of a permanent appointment in Snowlake were fading fast. She took a quick sip of sherry. 'Do you live with Clayte, then?' she asked, because that was the only thing she could think of that would explain Josephine's familiarity with the affairs of the Willow Inn.

'Nope. We'd drive each other crazy in no time rattling around in that fancy penthouse of his. Live in LA, though. See a lot of him. Reminds me of his father, God rest his soul.'

'Ms McGuigan——'

'Aunt Josephine to you.'

'Thank you. Aunt Josephine—now that you're here, what is it you'd like me to do for you?' This was all becoming too much for Georgina, but she supposed Clayte's aunt must have some purpose behind this extraordinary visitation.

'Don't want you to do anything, gal. Seen all I want to see, and I'm taking the next plane back to civilisation. Mind you, I'm just a nosy old woman. If Clayton had any sense, which of course he hasn't, he'd make you his wife, not his manager.' She chuckled. 'Maybe a bit of both. He needs managing.'

Georgina choked into her sherry. 'I don't think he wants a wife,' she muttered when she'd recovered her breath. 'And certainly not one like me. He's deathly afraid of apple pies. And he doesn't like picket fences either.'

'I know. As I said, no sense. Always goes for gals who look as though they've been cut out of some ridiculous fashion feature. The kind who know how to order designer dresses, but wouldn't know a needle if they saw one. Not his fault, though. It was that mother of his— Vanessa. Died a couple of years ago, poor fool.'

'Oh,' said Georgina, beginning to wonder if she was the one going senile. 'He—Clayte's never told me much about his mother.'

'Huh. Not surprised. That boy came to hate just about everything she stood for in the end.'

'Oh. Um—what did she stand for?' Georgina was still out of her depth.

'Cleanliness and keeping up appearances, that's what. Even used to hose down the road outside their house. Every day. Couldn't stand dirt of any kind. Made young Clayton sit with his chest touching the edge of the table so he wouldn't spill a crumb on the floor. Never allowed his friends to visit in case they tracked in mud or put sticky fingers on her model walls. Made him eat all his meals at home, though. Suppose she had to act the part of the perfect mother, and that meant preparing perfect meals.' Aunt Josephine shook her head disgustedly. '*And* knitting endless perfect sweaters. My poor Clive—he was Clayton's father—told me all about it. Nearly drove him crazy, that woman did. But by the time I met him he'd given up and left her. Clayton couldn't leave, of course. Not until he finished his schooling.'

She paused to draw breath. 'Still, he was a good boy when it comes right down to it. Always made sure his mother didn't want for a thing. Didn't have an easy childhood, though.' Josephine grinned suddenly, showing a set of very white teeth. 'Not easy for Vanessa either. He was a little hellion in spite of all she did to tame him down. Or maybe because of. Independent, self-willed, determined to do everything his way. He saw what knuckling under all the time had ended up doing to his father, so he made damn sure he didn't knuckle under himself.'

'Yes,' said Georgina. 'I can see how an upbringing like that could iron out most of the softness and leave just the sharp edges showing.' Her visitor only grunted, so she added doubtfully, 'Can I get you another glass of port?'

'Nope. Plane to catch. Seen what I wanted to see.' Aunt Josephine rose majestically to her feet. 'Got your head screwed on, you have. I can tell. Clayton could do a lot worse. Unfortunately he's too damn pigheaded to see it. Says if he ever gets married it'll be to a woman who can't cook or sew and wouldn't know a vacuum cleaner if it ate her. Not that he means to marry at all.'

Flinging her cape dramatically round her shoulders, Aunt Josephine stalked towards the door. Georgina followed, rubbing her eyes and feeling as if she'd been hit by a large, but surprisingly soft tank.

It wasn't until the end of an exhausting day, as she sat in her office clearing up odds and ends, that the full implications of Josephine McGuigan's visit really hit her.

For one thing, she now had a much clearer understanding of the forces that had made Clayte who and what he was. Also, it sounded as though he continued to think of her as drab little Mrs Clean, an obstinate thorn in his flesh whom he had hired in a moment of aberration. Which meant that as soon as the obligatory three months were up he was likely to pick up the phone and fire her from long distance with no further discussion on the matter. Or of getting Fred Charlton to do it.

Georgina slumped back in her chair. Suddenly the future seemed very bleak and grey. Not only might she shortly be out of a job, she would also be out of a dream. A dream that up until this instant she had steadfastly refused to acknowledge.

She groaned softly and covered her face with her hands, because this unadmitted and totally improbable fantasy was that Clayte would return to Snowlake, take

her in his arms and ask her to become his wife. Her
mouth twisted painfully. Ask? No, not Clayte. Order
would be more like it.

Except that it wasn't going to happen.

She had always known that, of course, which was why
she'd hidden her feelings from herself for so long. But
somehow the advent of his impossibly opinionated, de-
liciously dramatic aunt had succeeded in forcing the
blinkers from her eyes.

She loved that arrogant, aggressive, maddening and
surprisingly honourable man more than she loved anyone
in the world. She wasn't sure why, or how, it had come
about. But it had. And it was hopeless. Clayte would
never love a woman like her, let alone marry her. He
thought she was dull and domesticated—capable enough,
but not his type, and a little too obstinate to suit him.
Oh, maybe he wasn't totally immune to her, but he had
spent the night on her sofa without making the smallest
attempt to infiltrate her bed. And that last day he had
rejected her advances as if he were taking matches from
a child.

Besides, even if the impossible happened, she couldn't
afford to love a man to whom roots meant nothing, who
might expect her to pack her bags and move with him
whenever he opened a new hotel or decided to buy a new
penthouse. She couldn't live her childhood again. She
just couldn't.

Not that she would have to. Because there was no hope
that Clayte would ever ask her. Why should he? She'd
heard all the rumours of his conquests. They fairly sizzled
through the hotel grapevine. There was no reason
for him to settle for one, rather ordinary woman
who baked pies.

Georgina closed her eyes to the light. Life would go on and, as always, she would make the best of it.

When Jill came in a few minutes later, she found Georgina seated at her desk signing letters. Only her employer's parchment-white knuckles, and the fact that she had signed each letter twice and the blotter once, betrayed that all was not sunshine in the Kettrick universe.

'Hi, Georgi. Hope I'm not interrupting.'

Georgina shook her head at the portly young man with the thinning hair who stood on her doorstep holding an empty cup. 'No, I've just finished washing my hair. What are you collecting for, Gordon?'

'Isabel's cake. She sent me to borrow some sugar.'

'Come on in.' Georgina took the cup from her ex-husband, who followed her obediently into the kitchen, and began to spoon sugar out of a primrose-yellow canister on the counter. The doorbell rang just as she was handing it back.

'Expecting company?' asked Gordon.

'No.' She frowned. 'Bother.'

'What's the matter?'

Georgina sighed. 'Nothing much. But it's probably Tom Snape again. He's a salesman, and he's been trying to get us to order his company's cleaning products for months. Just lately he's been asking me out. I think he has some idea that sex may work better than his sales pitch.'

'And I assume it won't?' Gordon scratched his forehead and looked doubtful.

'Not a chance. You haven't met Tom Snape. Listen, will you do me a favour?'

'Depends. What is it?'

'If you see a tall, dark man through the peephole, will you answer the door for me? Then I'll come up behind you and you can put your arm around me. That way he'll think you're my boyfriend. If I'm lucky, it may put him off. Nothing else has.'

'Not even that grubby white sweatshirt and jeans?' Gordon cast a disapproving eye at her working clothes.

'Especially not those. For some reason Tom likes me in jeans.'

'He does? OK, shouldn't be difficult.' Gordon grinned. 'I *was* your boyfriend once. It'll be just like old times.'

For one brief moment Georgina's mind went back to those old times. She had loved Gordon, and his defection had left her with a great reluctance to love again. Yet all she felt for him now was a vague, almost maternal fondness. That, of course, was why it had been so easy to move next door.

'Behave yourself,' she chided him now, knowing very well he was teasing, and that he had no more interest in her than she had in him. Fortunately, her ex was devoted to his wife.

The bell rang again, more insistently, and Gordon sauntered over to the door. 'Yes?' Georgina heard him say, in a deliberately surly voice. 'What do you want?'

Smiling to herself, she hurried out to join him, and at once Gordon turned towards her and dropped a possessive arm around her waist.

'Hello, darling,' he growled sexily. 'Finished washing your hair?'

'Yes, I——' Georgina broke off with a sense that she'd just been kicked in the chest. Her heart plummeted down to somewhere in the region of her knees. It wasn't Tom

Snape who stood on the step glowering like a bull about to charge a china shop.

It was Clayton O'Neill.

CHAPTER SEVEN

CLAYTE'S slashing gaze travelled over Georgina as if she were a particularly repellent blister. 'Well, well,' he drawled, in a husky baritone that made all her nerve-ends vibrate, 'what have we here? A cosy little *ménage à deux?*'

Georgina stopped feeling stunned and embarrassed as indignation began to stiffen all her muscles. What right had Clayte to take that tone with her? It was Saturday afternoon, she was on her own time, and her private life was none of his business. Even if Gordon wasn't really her private life.

'Gordon, this is Clayton O'Neill, my boss,' she said frigidly. 'Mr O'Neill, this is my—friend, Gordon.'

'Friend?' repeated Clayte, raising a derisive black eyebrow. 'I suppose that's one way of putting it.'

Gordon glanced quickly from the large man scowling on the doorstep to Georgina's flushed and angry face. 'Er—sugar,' he murmured. 'Better get it back to Isabel. She'll be waiting.'

'Gordon, wait,' cried Georgina desperately. 'There's no need——'

'Think there is,' Gordon interrupted. 'Can see you and your—um—boss have things to talk about. And it's time for me to feed the pigeons.' He pushed past Clayte and hurried down the pathway to the gate.

'Pigeons?' said Clayte, staring after him. 'From the looks of it he's already serviced one pigeon. Does the man go in for multiple lofts?'

118

Georgina tightened her lips. 'What's that supposed to mean?' she asked dangerously.

He turned back to her, still with that scornful glitter in his eyes. 'I'd have thought it was obvious.'

'Well, it's not. Perhaps you'd care to explain.'

'Perhaps I would. If you'd care to ask me in.'

Georgina didn't want to ask him in. There was something in the way he held his body, in the hardness of his eyes and the grim, almost cruel set of his mouth that she didn't trust. This contemptuous stranger wasn't the man she loved.

But he *had* spent the night in her home once—and no harm had come to her... Besides, this scene had to be played out to its conclusion.

She stepped back, and he stalked past her into the cottage.

'Have a seat,' she said coolly.

'A seat? Surely your last guest was offered more—shall we say—*stimulating* accommodation?'

Georgina saw red. She hadn't seen Clayte for over two months, and somewhere along the line she had discovered that she loved him quite hopelessly. Now, at last, he was back, taunting her as if she'd committed some unspeakable crime—for no other reason than that her ex-husband had turned up to borrow a cup of sugar.

'Listen,' she said, facing him with her hands on her hips, 'I've had enough of this, Clayte. What I choose to do on my own time is my business, and you have no right whatever to come charging in here like a mad bull and suggest that——'

'Suggest what, Georgina?' His hands were on his hips too as he turned to face her, and she took in that for once, instead of wearing a suit, he was dressed in skin-hugging jeans and a purple shirt. Even in her fury she couldn't help thinking that there weren't many men who could wear purple and still look quite savagely male. But Clayte could.

'You're accusing me of sleeping with Gordon, aren't you?' she demanded.

'Sleeping?' he said silkily. 'I don't know much about that.'

Georgina clenched her teeth. She wouldn't deny his insinuations. Why should she? Whom she slept with, or whether she slept with anyone, was not his affair.

'What do you want?' she asked baldly, hoping she sounded as surly as Gordon had when he'd asked precisely that same question.

Clayte slapped a deliberate hand against his thigh. 'I'm not sure. What are you offering?'

'Tea?' she suggested with icy sweetness.

He shook his head. 'No. I don't think so.' As Georgina watched, she saw his jaw harden, and knew that he'd made a decision. When he took a purposeful step towards her, she moved back, but was stopped when her legs came up against the sofa.

'What's the matter, Georgina?' he asked, extending an arm to curve his hand round the back of her neck. 'Are your favours reserved for your ex-husband? He *is* your ex, I presume? I wonder what his wife thinks of that?' He pushed his fingers up through her still damp hair, and in spite of herself Georgina felt excitement shiver down her spine.

No, she thought urgently. No. She was not going to give in to Clayte just as if she were truly the unprincipled wanton he thought her.

'Please take your hand off me,' she said frozenly.

At once he dropped his arm to his side. 'Sorry,' he taunted. 'I didn't realise you were a one-man woman.'

Quite suddenly Georgina's fury evaporated, turned to a kind of weary despair. She *was* a one-man woman. Unfortunately the man in question was about as inaccessible to her as the moon, even if, at this moment, she could reach out and touch him if she chose. Perhaps it wasn't surprising that Clayte had jumped to the conclusion he had. She had intended Tom Snape to be deceived. It was just unfortunate that Clayte hadn't turned out to be Tom.

'Gordon isn't mine,' she told him, sinking down on to the sofa. 'He's Isabel's.' It wasn't important to maintain her pride any longer. It was only important to be honest.

'I agree. Too bad for his wife you didn't think of that earlier.' He was standing over her now with his fists balled against his thighs, and looking very much like the enraged bull she had accused him of resembling.

Georgina passed a hand across her eyes. 'Clayte,' she said tiredly, 'why are you behaving like this? There's nothing between me and Gordon, but even if there was I don't understand why you should care.'

When he didn't answer she looked up, and for a moment she could have sworn she read confusion in the dark glance he angled her way. Then his face seemed to close up again. 'I don't like cheats,' he replied.

'Neither do I.'

'Or liars.'

Georgina felt her anger come to the boil again, but she forced it back ruthlessly. There was no point in allowing Clayte to provoke her. It would solve nothing.

'I am neither a cheat nor a liar,' she said steadily. 'I've told you the truth.'

'Is that so? Which means that as far as you're concerned there's nothing wrong with letting another woman's husband cuddle up to you—and call you "darling".'

Georgina stifled a desire to burst into hysterical laughter. 'Nothing at all,' she agreed glibly. 'Not when the other woman's husband is my ex—who happened to be doing me a favour.'

'Even in a town the size of Snowlake I'd have thought you could find plenty of unattached men to supply you with that sort of favour.'

The contempt in his voice made her wince, and she decided that this ridiculous misunderstanding had been allowed to go on quite long enough. 'You were supposed to be Tom Snape,' she said, not looking at him. 'He works for a hotel supplier and he's been pestering me to go out with him for weeks. I don't want to. Isabel sent Gordon over to borrow a cup of sugar, and when the doorbell rang I asked him to pretend to be my boyfriend. Now please go, Clayte.'

There was dead silence in the room, then after a while Georgina felt the springs of the sofa shift under her as Clayte lowered himself down beside her. 'Your ex did a good job,' he said gruffly. 'Is that the truth?'

'Of course it is.' She fixed her gaze on the new clock she had bought for her mantel, and noticed with faint surprise that somehow the afternoon had passed her by. It was already past five o'clock.

'Hmm.'

No regrets or explanations, just that gruff, 'Hmm.' But she felt his hand on her cheek turning her gently to face him, and when she looked into his eyes she had all the apology she needed.

'Why did it matter to you?' she asked.

With his free hand he curled a lock of her hair around his finger. 'I suppose,' he admitted, 'it mattered because if you were in need of any favours of that nature I wanted to be the one to provide them.'

'I . . .' she swallowed '. . . I don't understand.'

'Oh, yes, you do. One thing you are not, Mrs Kettrick, is stupid.' He shifted his body closer, and she felt the lean length of his thigh against her leg.

Georgina gulped. 'But—you said you didn't approve of—of——'

'Making love to my managers? I don't. But I'm a man, Georgina, and somehow you've succeeded in working your way under my skin. You're an itch that just won't go away.'

'Calamine lotion,' she said breathlessly.

'What?'

'Calamine lotion. It's good for itches.'

'Not this kind of itch.' He moved his hand from her cheek and placed it over her hip.

'Clayte,' she whispered, 'is this why you came back? To—to——'

'To take you to bed? Perhaps. Among other things. Are you agreeable?'

'You make it sound like a business transaction,' she told him, wondering if the wry tilt to his lips meant that he was laughing at her again.

He shrugged. 'What's wrong with that? Business is what I do best.' When she only gazed at him with a puzzled frown, he added with much less detachment, 'Georgina, I won't make you any promises I can't keep.'

No, of course he wouldn't. But if she let him do what he asked, what her own blood was crying out for him to do, it would only be a thousand times harder to bear it when he left. And yet—and yet . . .

'Clayte,' she said, 'I can't——'

He placed a finger over her lips. 'It's all right. You don't have to.'

He still sounded cool and businesslike. But the hand that was massaging her hip wasn't cool. It was warm and firm, moving in slow, delicious circles that sent a million tingling messages to her brain.

'What—other things?' she asked, in a frantic effort to take her mind off those messages.

'Other things?'

'You—you said you'd come back to take me to bed—among other things.'

'Ah. Yes.' The movement of his hand ceased abruptly. 'I said *perhaps* I'd come back with that very appealing purpose in mind, although I don't think I was particularly aware of it. What I actually came back for was to fire you.'

Georgina gasped, took a deep breath and jumped up as if he'd jabbed her with a pin. 'You could have done that by phone,' she said coldly, hoping she sounded a lot more controlled than she felt. Pride, after all, mattered very much.

'I know. I chose not to. It seemed—gutless.'

'I doubt you'll ever lack guts, Mr O'Neill.' She reverted to formality automatically. 'May I ask *why* you're not satisfied with my performance?'

'Oh, I'm very satisfied. Not a single rumour of graft or inefficiency. But your three months happen to be up. Or will be shortly.'

'I know. But if you're satisfied, why——?'

'Because you're a woman, Mrs Kettrick.'

Oh, yes, she was a woman all right. Georgina stared down at him sprawled at ease on her sofa, saw the denim pull tight across his thighs. Then she raised her eyes to his face. 'That statement, Mr O'Neill, may very well be grounds for a lawsuit.'

His lips twisted. 'You would sue me too, wouldn't you?'

'If I had to. Sexual discrimination is against the law. As it should be.'

'I agree. However, that wasn't precisely my meaning.'

'Oh?' Georgina glared at him. How dared he look so relaxed and unaffected—and sexy—while he sat there passing judgement on her future? 'You mean there's some other interpretation to the declaration that you intend to fire me because I'm a woman?'

'As a matter of fact there is. Sit down, Georgina.' He patted the empty space beside him.

'Why? So you can maul me some more? Before you fire me?'

His mouth tightened. 'No, so I can talk to you without wondering if you're about to pick up the poker and break it over my head.'

'Why didn't *I* think of that?' muttered Georgina.

'I'm surprised you didn't. Come on, Medusa, stop glowering at me as if you'd like to turn me into stone.' He took her hand, gave it a firm tug, and before she was able to stop him he had pulled her down beside him and had both hands on her shoulders so that she couldn't move. 'Now listen to me,' he said.

'All right. I'm listening.' What else was there to do? Besides, in spite of everything, she liked the feel of him there, liked his spicy breath, and the pressure of his knee touching hers.

'Good. The reason I decided not to keep you beyond your probationary three months was that I've been finding it increasingly difficult to get you out of my mind. As long as you remained my employee I didn't see the problem going away. Particularly not once Aunt Josephine had you in her sights as the next Mrs Clayton O'Neill. The neat and uncomplicated solution seemed to be to eliminate the cause of my distraction. I prefer simplicity in my business dealings, don't you?'

'I am not,' said Georgina, 'a business dealing. As you've already pointed out, I'm a person. A female one. I actually have feelings, Clayte O'Neill.'

'I know.' He smiled ruefully, and suddenly he didn't look hard and insensitive any more, he looked warm and seductive and irresistible. 'That's exactly why I made up my mind to get rid of you—the other alternative being to take you to bed.'

Georgina licked her lips. 'What made you think that was an option?'

'You did—when you offered yourself to me so nicely before I left. Just as well I had a plane to catch, wasn't it?'

'Oh! Do you mean if you hadn't——?'

'No.' He withdrew his hands and flung himself back against the sofa. 'No. Apart from the fact that I meant it when I said I don't conduct affairs with my staff, I found I genuinely didn't want to hurt you.'

'Oh, really? Is that the kind of lovemaking you go in for? The kinky kind? I wouldn't have thought it.' Up until now, the pain she had been trying to ignore had been a throbbing ache. Now, all of a sudden, it threatened to boil up and engulf her, and she felt a desperate need to strike back—to make Clayte suffer just as she was suffering.

Just for a moment, she thought she might have succeeded too well. He stopped staring straight ahead and turned to look at her. Then he put a hand on the back of her head and forced it towards him so that her face was almost touching his. 'Watch it,' he said. 'It's been a long day and I've never been noted for my forbearance. Don't give me ideas.'

'You petrify me,' she scoffed. He didn't, though. There was a look in his eyes she didn't understand— almost as if he really was hurting.

But Clayte was a man who seemed unwilling to acknowledge even the possibility of pain. 'Do I?' he said, releasing her and resting his arm along the back of the sofa. 'On the whole I'd rather make love to you. But that would put us back to square one.'

Georgina shook her head. 'Clayte, stop talking in riddles. Are you firing me or not?'

He raked a hand through his hair. 'No. I thought I was. It seemed the kindest and most sensible thing to do.'

'Kindest? I can see sensible, but...'

'Georgina, for God's sake...' His voice was rasping and impatient as usual. 'Don't you realise the inevitable outcome if I keep you on?'

She knew what he meant. Why pretend she didn't? And he was right. If she continued to work for him, sooner or later he would get exactly what he had quite frankly admitted he wanted.

'Why,' she said carefully, 'should that concern you? Apart from your scruples about fraternising with staff, I'd expect it to solve your problem for you. You know— the irritating itch.'

'Georgina...' He caught her upper arms and his black eyes seemed to staple her to the back of the sofa. 'Georgina, don't be obtuse. Bending my own rules might solve my problem. But you've made it very clear that it wouldn't solve anything for you.'

'Does that matter?'

'Oddly enough, it seems to.'

'Oh.' She stared back at him, desperate to conceal the true state of her emotions. It was bad enough that Clayte knew she would be putty in his hands. But for some reason it was even more humiliating that he also had an inkling of how deeply her feelings were involved—as his obviously weren't, except on a very superficial level. The only reason he said he didn't want to hurt her was that damaging her psyche wouldn't sit well with his conscience. At least he has one, she thought bitterly. But Clayte didn't know what to do with a woman like her. His first instinct simply had been to eliminate her from his orbit because she wasn't a good-time girl who gave lightly, took lightly, then moved easily on to pastures new. That sort of woman he understood.

Georgina didn't want him to think she was some kind of clinging vine who would be devastated if he loved her and left her—for all she would be.

'Clayte,' she said, all of a sudden incredibly conscious of the inflexible grip of his hands around her arms. 'Clayte, I have the occasional itch too.' It wasn't what she'd meant to say, but somehow the words had spilled out.

Surprise flickered across his features, followed by startled amusement. 'Do you?' he said. 'Yes, I suppose I'd figured that out, but I thought...' He shook his head slowly. 'Perhaps I had it all wrong. Are you making me an offer, Mrs Kettrick? It's a much more attractive one than tea.'

'I...' Georgina swallowed hard. *Was* she making him an offer? If she was, it would have to be without any girlish illusions about the future. Clayte would never be an apple-pie man.

He was smiling now, that full-lipped, rawly sexual smile that showed his teeth, and his dark eyes were undressing her very slowly, peeling off the stained white sweatshirt, unfastening her jeans, easing them down over her hips...

She gasped and sat up very straight. 'What are you doing?' she asked unsteadily.

He showed rather more of his teeth. 'Nothing. Is there something you'd like me to do?'

Georgina stared at him. He had asked her something of the sort once before. And yes, there was something she would like him to do. Something that was all she could ever hope for from this man.

So why not?

In her heart she knew very well why not, but all the same, because she couldn't stop herself, she put her hand on his chest and began to undo the buttons of his purple shirt. Just for a few seconds, Clayte's features darkened, and he sat totally still, holding her grey gaze with his black one. Then he let his breath out very slowly and moved both hands to her waist.

'Georgina,' he said in a voice that seemed to flow over her skin like heated honey, 'are you sure?'

No, she wasn't sure. Strangely, she had a feeling that he wasn't either. All the same, somewhere in the course of this incredible evening a match had been struck, and it had started a conflagration whose progress could have only one end.

'I'm sure that you and I are meant to happen,' she said, burying both hands in the dark hair waving on his neck—the hair that she had yearned and yet resisted the urge to touch for so long. 'And I'm sure I want to. Do you——?'

Clayte cut off her words with a groan as he covered her mouth with his lips and bent her backwards so that she was half lying, half sitting on the sofa, with her head pressed against the padded arm and her feet still just touching the floor.

'More than I've ever wanted anything in my life,' he murmured, as though he couldn't quite believe what he was saying.

She felt his lips on her neck now, and his magical hands were pushing up her sweatshirt, easing it over her head to expose not a flimsily seductive strip of lace and satin, but her very practical white cotton bra. She knew a moment's confusion as she heard Clayte's muffled exclamation, and then it didn't matter any more because the bra wasn't there, and his mouth was invoking wonderful, unbelievably erotic sensations in her breasts.

She pulled the purple shirt out of its belt and felt the smooth silkiness touch her knuckles as she ran her palms over the hard expanse of his back. Then he was doing all those things she had read in his eyes, and her jeans were being tugged below her hips. She reached for his belt buckle.

After that there were no barriers between them, and Clayte's arm was beneath her thighs stretching her full-length on the sofa as he leaned over her and, with surprising gentleness, stroked the soft hair back from her face.

'You're beautiful,' he said huskily. 'So unbearably beautiful, my Georgina. I can't believe——'

Georgina never heard what he couldn't believe, because at that moment he began to lower his body on to hers, and as he extended his left leg to trap her between his thighs his foot hit the arm of the sofa. He swore softly, put his arm around her, and tumbled her on to the floor.

'That's better,' he whispered, running a tantalising finger down her spine. 'Your sofa was never intended for serious merging. Besides, I could never see myself making love to a woman on a flowerbed.'

Georgina giggled. 'How about a pink plush rug?' She gasped as he pulled her on top of him and slid both hands very slowly over her rear.

'It'll have to do,' he growled.

And do it did. She had half expected that Clayte, with his businesslike outlook and determination to get what needed doing done, would be the kind of man who made love quickly and thoroughly before moving on to other, more important matters. But he wasn't. He did indeed love her thoroughly, but with infinite care to give her as much pleasure as she hoped with all her heart she was giving him—even though, except for a few incredible moments when she knew an ecstasy beyond all possible dreams, the knowledge was never far from her mind that this might be the only time they would be together like this. The only time she would know love as it was truly meant to be—two separate individuals who wanted only to make each other happy.

In the final enchanted moment, Georgina cried out Clayte's name.

It was some time afterwards, as she lay with her head resting on his chest, that she realised his thoughts were no longer with her. He was gazing steadily up at the ceiling, and his body was not relaxed as it had been when their passion was spent. He seemed to be searching for the answer to an insoluble problem, and Georgina had the odd feeling that in some inexplicable way she had lost him.

'Clayte?' she murmured. 'Is something wrong?'

He tightened his. arm around her and abstractedly began to knead her shoulder. 'There are times,' he replied obliquely, 'when I almost wish I hadn't given up smoking.'

Georgina pushed herself up on one elbow and stared down at him. 'You used to smoke?'

'Mmm. When I was young and foolish, I had an idea that cigarettes aided my thought processes.'

'What they actually do is smell and make a mess,' said Georgina flatly. 'They don't make you think.'

'I suppose you also regard them as filthy, immoral and unclean,' said Clayte, with such bitterness that she knew she had said the wrong thing.

'What is it you need to think about?' she asked. 'Something *is* wrong, isn't it?'

'Yes.' He sprang abruptly to his feet and began to pull on his jeans. 'You're shivering. I'll fetch a blanket.'

Was she shivering? She supposed she must be, but although it was late September she hadn't been aware of feeling cold.

Clayte disappeared, and a moment later came back carrying the afghan from the end of her bed. 'Here,' he said, tossing it at her. 'Wrap yourself in that.'

Obediently, Georgina did as he said and sat up. Clayte walked over to the window, and she watched the evening sun touch his bare shoulders with its fire. His skin turned to a deep, burning gold as he pressed his fists down on the sill and stared into the gathering shadows.

'What is it, Clayte?' she repeated.

He didn't answer at once, and when he did he sounded angry. 'What should be wrong? I came here to solve a problem, and ended up causing one instead.'

'I'm sorry I'm a problem,' said Georgina, feeling a small chill steal over her heart.

He moved his head impatiently. 'It's not your fault.'

'All right,' she said, choosing her words with care. 'Then what, precisely, is the matter?' She stood up, pulling the afghan tightly around her body. 'Are you regretting what happened just because I'm a member of your staff?'

He shrugged. 'That's part of it. Believe me, I didn't intend anything to happen.'

Georgina did believe him. 'It doesn't matter,' she said with as much conviction as she could manage. 'I can always find another job.' In spite of her efforts, it was hard to keep the hurt from her voice.

He swung round to face her, his mouth twisted in a curious grimace. 'Oh, sure. And what then? Do I fly into Snowlake when it happens to suit me, make use of your beautiful body, and fly off again? Is that what you're suggesting?'

'Is that what you want?' The look on his face made her take a quick step away from him.

'Of course,' he sneered. 'Wouldn't any man?'

Georgina sat down on the sofa. 'You don't mean that, do you?' she said quietly.

Clayte leaned on the sill, and rested the back of his head against the window. 'I don't know what I mean,' he replied. 'Except that, yes, of course I want to make love to you again. No woman has ever——' He broke off, then added savagely, 'And of course I want you available. Are you prepared to take me on those terms?'

'No.'

He laughed, a hard, grating laugh that made her wince. 'I didn't think so. So what do you suggest we do?'

Georgina knew that the obvious solution wouldn't occur to him. He wasn't interested in marriage, especially to a woman like her. She felt the chill in her heart grow deeper, more pervasive, and she hugged the afghan round her for protection. 'I suggest,' she said sadly, 'that you do what you came up here to do.'

'Fire you?'

She nodded. 'Yes. Then you can go back to Los Angeles and forget me.'

'Not a chance,' he said harshly. 'Even if I could forget you, do you think Aunt Josephine would let me?'

Aunt Josephine. In the midst of her misery, Georgina felt a brief lightening of her heart, and the ghost of a smile formed on her lips. 'No,' she admitted. 'I should think it's highly unlikely.'

When she looked up, Clayte was smiling too. It was a grim sort of smile, but still a smile.

'You see,' he said. 'The whole thing's impossible, isn't it? I want you. But you want a man who is willing to give you the kind of life you've worked so hard for—a man you can bake your damn pies for in this town full of tourists and water. I can't handle that, Georgina.'

'You can't handle Snowlake? Or—or marriage?'

He gave an exasperated snort and strode across the room to sit beside her. 'Marriage? I never considered...' He picked up her hand and began to rub his thumb across her palm. 'I'm not the marrying kind, Georgina. I told you that a long time ago.'

Georgina breathed deeply. 'I know. But there are other, less binding commitments.'

Clayte shook his head. 'No. Not for you, there aren't. And I can't see myself locked into any kind of domestic arrangement, even the less binding kind. I'm sorry, but——' He stopped when he caught sight of her face, very pale in the fast fading dusk. 'Georgina, don't look at me like that. You're happy here in Snowlake. You feel secure in the first stable home you've ever known. What right have I to ask you to give that up for a man who doesn't value the things you value? Who would lose his temper every time he saw you in an apron?'

Georgina smiled wanly, and said with a break in her voice, 'You've the right to ask anything you want, Clayte. Just as I have the right to say no.'

'And would you?'

'Are you asking?'

He put a finger under her chin and lifted it up. 'I want you, Georgina,' he said roughly. 'I want you with me, so that I can make love to you every night and every morning. But no, I'm not asking, because in the end I'd only make you unhappy. The least I can do is leave you to live your life in peace.'

Peace, thought Georgina. After this evening, what kind of peace can I expect to find without you? But there was no point in saying that to him. Clayte hadn't said he loved her, only that he wanted her. At least, here in Snowlake, she had friends who cared about her, and a home where she felt happy and safe. Or had up until the break-in. Now she didn't feel quite as safe as before. But there could be no security with Clayte either unless he loved her. If there was even a chance...

'Clayte,' she asked, 'if I said I was willing to leave Snowlake, would you take me?'

He dropped her hand. 'No,' he said. 'I know you don't think much of me sometimes, but I'm not totally without decent feelings.'

'I see,' she replied. 'And yet you had no problem with the idea of coming up here to tell me I was out of a job.'

'No. No problem at all. I have contacts here. One of them had already agreed to take you on. As a favour to me.'

'I see,' said Georgina again, wishing his re-arrangement of her future didn't make her feel as if he'd just plunged a knife into her heart. 'Neat but brutal. And now?'

'And now,' he said, standing up and stalking back to the window, 'now, my sweet Georgina, it's up to you.'

She stared at the shape of his back outlined in the pale silver light. 'What's up to me?'

'The decision as to where you want to work.'

Oh. That decision. 'You mean I can stay on as your manager if I choose to? Or else transfer to another hotel?'

'Yup.'

'Oh. But you said——'

'I know what I said. I've changed my mind.'

He was still facing the window, and it was impossible to tell from his words whether her answer was important to him or not. When she started to murmur, 'But——' again, he interrupted.

'Georgina, listen to me. The fact is, I no longer feel justified in arranging matters entirely to suit my own convenience. So if you want to hang on to your job at the Willow Inn...' he shrugged '...it's yours. You've proved you can do it, and there's no real reason why Fred Charlton, my assistant, can't deal with most of the details. It's unlikely I'll need to trouble you again.'

He spoke with such crisp matter-of-factness that Georgina could hardly believe this was the same man who, less than an hour before, had loved her so tenderly—so beautifully.

'I'll think about it,' she said, bending down to pick up her clothes. 'Right now I'm going to get dressed.'

Clayte turned from the window, but she ignored him and padded into her bedroom still clutching the afghan around her. For a moment she stared dully at her face in the big old-fashioned mirror. It seemed paler and smaller than usual. She started to pull on a sweatshirt, then changed her mind and hurried into the bathroom. Under the hot, comforting stream of the shower, gradually her heart, and every part of her, began very painfully to thaw—and she knew that all her worst fears had been confirmed.

Loving Clayte had not been a mistake, it had been as inevitable as the rising of the moon. But it had solved nothing, and now, when he left, her days would be emptier, more lonely than they had ever been before. She had known loneliness in the past in all those nameless towns she had passed through with her parents, but that loneliness would be nothing compared to her life without Clayte. Now she would have to learn to live the rest of her days with what might have been.

She wrapped herself in a towel and went back into the bedroom. Clayte, still in the living-room, made no sound.

Vaguely, she wondered what she would have said had he asked her to go with him to Los Angeles. Not that he would, of course. His principles wouldn't allow him to uproot her for what, as far as he was concerned, could only be a temporary arrangement. As she shrugged herself into a pale green dressing-gown, she thought grudgingly that she had to respect him for that.

But did that mean she could continue to work at the Willow Inn? Or would she be better advised to accept his offer of a job at another hotel? Oddly, at this moment, it didn't seem to matter much either way.

She went back into the living-room. It was getting late, and although food was the last thing on her mind she was sure Clayte would see no reason to let emotion come between him and his evening meal.

But he wasn't in the living-room. She checked the kitchen, and then the bathroom. He wasn't there either, so she started at the beginning and searched the cottage all over again. She called his name. No answer. His clothes were gone too.

After a while, the truth hit her. Clayte, with his hard-headed dedication to clean and clear-cut decision-making, had decided to walk cleanly out of her life.

CHAPTER EIGHT

AT FIRST, as Georgina stood in the darkened room and stared out of the window at the trees, she didn't really believe it. Clayte couldn't have walked out on her like that without even taking the time to say goodbye. Oh, she knew he could be brutal on occasion, but surely...

Stop it, Georgina. She interrupted her futile speculations ruthlessly. There had never been much point in trying to figure out what made Clayton O'Neill do the things he did. He was gone, and that was all there was to it.

Shaking her head, she turned to face a room that suddenly seemed emptied of life. Because there was no reason to remain standing, she sank down on to the floor, where her gaze came to rest on the rumpled shape of the pink plush rug beside the sofa. In this light it looked black, like a boulder. She supposed she would have to give it away now, because she didn't think she could live with its constant reminder...

'Georgina? What the devil are you doing sitting in the dark?'

Georgina jumped as the light flashed on and she looked up to see Clayte standing by the door. Her heart began to flutter, and automatically she put a hand over it to conceal its erratic beat from his sharp gaze. He was glowering down at her as if he thought she owed him an explanation.

She owed *him*...?

Her lethargy and regret fell away as if they'd never existed, and she scrambled on to her feet. 'And what do *you* mean by disappearing like a conjuror's rabbit?' she demanded. 'I thought you'd walked out on me.'

'Without even saying goodbye? Is that the kind of man you think I am?'

His voice was hard, accusing. He actually thought he had a right to be angry. Well, so did she. She'd gone from despair to ecstasy to despair again, all in the course of one evening. He was the cause, and she was in no mood to take any more of it.

'I've given up trying to figure out what kind of man you are,' she snapped. 'All I know is that when I came to look for you you'd gone.'

Clayte ran a hand round the back of his neck, and when he replied his tone was peculiarly flat. 'So that is what you thought. It's just as well I'm leaving, then, isn't it?'

Georgina felt a pricking at the back of her eyes. She blinked several times. 'I suppose it is. Where were you?' she asked coldly.

'In the garden. Didn't you notice I'd left the door unlocked?'

No, she hadn't, in spite of the fact that ever since the break-in she'd been acutely conscious of locks. 'You shouldn't have,' she said. 'You're the one who insisted on turning my home into a fortified camp in the first place.'

'I was right outside, keeping watch. Do you seriously think I'd take chances where your safety is concerned?'

He already had. But those were different chances, a different kind of safety. The kind she had already lost. 'I don't know what to think. What were you doing out there?'

He pushed his hands deep into his pockets and propped himself up against the wall. 'I needed air. And time to think.'

Georgina noticed that he looked extraordinarily tired. She glanced at the clock. 'You were out there for over half an hour.'

'So?'

'So—so I thought you'd gone.' Suddenly her tears wouldn't be held back, and she felt them begin to swim down her cheeks. She turned away at once so that he wouldn't see. But she wasn't quick enough.

In three strides he was across the room, sweeping her into his arms and pulling her round to face him. She buried her face in his shirt.

'Would it have mattered so much?' he asked softly. 'If I *had* gone?'

Didn't he know? Did he really not know that after what they had shared it would matter for the rest of her life?

'Yes,' she mumbled against the silky fabric. 'It would.'

He was silent for some time, and when he did speak it was only to say curtly, 'Then I'm sorry.'

He didn't sound very sorry, Georgina thought. But it had always been difficult to tell what Clayte was feeling beneath the abrasive front he presented to the world. She lifted her head, and when she saw his face, as uncompromising and immobile as a sculpture, she felt a great and urgent need to escape. But he wouldn't release her, and on an unexpected wave of frustration she lifted her fists and slammed them down on his chest.

Clayte swore with considerable proficiency and caught both her wrists in one hand. Then he bent his head and kissed her with such crushing ferocity that for a few seconds she didn't think she could breathe. But soon the kiss deepened, became pure passion, and Georgina felt her insides begin to melt. Slowly, and in spite of the pain in her heart, she lifted her arms and wound them around his neck.

At once Clayte swore again and held her away. 'Right,' he said, with unbearable detachment. 'I'm afraid this is getting us nowhere. What did you decide about the job?'

Just like that. Turn off the passion and let's get on with business. And the fact was, she hadn't decided anything. All the same, she heard herself saying quietly, 'I'd like to stay on at the Willow Inn.'

'Fine,' he agreed. 'That's settled, then. Now—I suppose we'd better get on with saying goodbye.'

Georgina gaped at him. He sounded utterly callous and uncaring—yet behind the hard black glaze of his eyes she thought she saw—what? An intensity of feeling that surely must mean something. There was desire there, certainly, but, oh, more than that...

'I—I don't know...' she whispered, totally at a loss for words.

Clayte shrugged, stepped back and spread his arms wide. 'Kiss me goodbye, Georgina,' he ordered, with an unusual roughness in his voice.

His purple shirt was damp from her tears, his dark hair falling seductively across his forehead. He looked wild, and wicked and irresistible. And she didn't want to kiss him goodbye, she wanted to pull him into her arms and never let him go, to fall with him on to the pink plush rug and make love to him until the birds sang in the morning.

But it was not to be.

Reluctantly she went up to him, placed her hands on his shoulders and, standing on tiptoe, touched her lips lightly to his cheek. When she felt his hands begin to circle her waist, she moved away.

Clayte stared down at her. His arms were folded on his chest now, and the look on his face had become as closed and forbidding as she had ever seen it.

He went on staring for a long time, and then he nodded, as if confirming something in his own mind. 'Yes,' he said. 'Perhaps that is for the best. Goodbye, Georgina.' He smiled at her, a white slit of a smile that somehow matched the terrible bleakness in his eyes. 'Shall I give your love to Aunt Josephine?'

'Yes. If you like.' The words came out as a mere whisper in the early evening air.

He looked at her for a few moments longer, the odd smile still distorting his virile features, and then he turned his back and headed for the door. 'Don't forget to lock it,' he said, in a voice that didn't sound as though it came from him at all. 'And—thank you.'

The door closed behind him, and Georgina thought she smelled the scent of fading roses in the night.

'Georgi, I think Harvey's having trouble in the bar.' Lori's soft voice halted Georgina as she hurried across the lobby on her way to a meeting with the Willow Inn's firm of accountants.

'What sort of trouble?' she asked. 'Surely not drunk and disorderly this early in the day?'

'I don't think so,' said Lori. 'Jenny said she heard Mrs Durham having hysterics.'

Georgina rolled up her eyes. Of course. The Durhams were back. They always took extra holidays in October, and Mrs Durham had been complaining in high gear almost from the moment she arrived.

She had started with the weather, which didn't suit her, moved on to the temperature of the bedrooms, which was sure to aggravate Mr Durham's lumbago, and then demanded to see the manager because there was a suspicious noise outside the bathroom window. The noise had turned out to be a bird. Later she had woken every other guest on her floor when she got up in the middle of the night and mistook Mr Durham's sponge-bag for a mouse.

'All right,' Georgina said to Lori. 'Could you call the boardroom and tell the accountants I'll be a minute or two late? Harvey's quite capable of coping, but he's got a short fuse on the subject of the Durhams, and I'd just as soon not have a scene.'

She made for the bar, wondering if a hysterical Dorothy Durham might be the straw that finally broke her control and reduced her to blubbering inanity.

It had been two weeks now since Clayte had left her with a polite, 'Thank you,' but only two days since Chef Alexander had remarked casually that he'd heard Mr O'Neill was involved with Vicki Romero, Hollywood's hottest young starlet. Georgina hadn't slept much since then, and her efforts to get her life back on track had so far met with utter failure. She felt strung out and on edge and at the same time deeply despondent. Even the news that two youths had admitted breaking into her cottage hadn't done a great deal to cheer her. Not surprisingly, they had long since disposed of her possessions.

All the same, as she hurried down the passage to the bar she reminded herself that sooner or later everything would fall into place. Experience had taught her that there was never any point in dwelling on the past, and one day the peace Clayte had promised to leave her in

would come. It would be a lonely peace, but she would
learn to sleep again—and to laugh.

Unfortunately there was nothing remotely amusing
about Mrs Durham at the top of her form. Which she
was now. Georgina could hear her as she approached
the scene of the disturbance.

'Oh! Oh! You're not really trying to tell me it wasn't
a fly? Of course it was a fly. In my drink. Don't you
think I know a fly when I see one? I'll never be able to
enjoy my gin again.'

'It was vodka, Dorothy.' Mr Durham's practised poli-
tician's voice rose firmly above his wife's shrieks. 'And
it wasn't a fly, it was a stray bit of ash from my pipe.'

'I assure you, madam...' Harvey's voice this time,
defending the reputation of the Inn.

Georgina groaned silently and entered the arena. A
trio of businessmen who had been discussing their bi-
cuspids over martinis stood up and marched grimly out
of the room.

'She's driving away my customers,' hissed Harvey in
a stage whisper.

'What! Oh, that's all you care about, isn't it?' Mrs
Durham turned wild, pink-rimmed eyes on Georgina.
'Mrs Kettrick, do you realise what's happened——?'

'Yes, indeed,' said Georgina briskly. 'I understand you
found some ash in your drink. How very unpleasant for
you. Now, since you've obviously had a nasty shock,
I'm sure you'll be wanting to take a rest. May I suggest
a little light lunch in your suite? Along with a complimentary bottle of wine? I'll be happy to arrange it for
you.'

'Well,' muttered Mrs Durham, dabbing at her eyes
with her hankie. 'Maybe...'

Georgina waited patiently for the grudging acquiescence that she knew would follow. The word 'complimentary' always had a soothing effect on the Durham nerves.

As Mr Durham led his wife from the bar, Georgina heard him growl, 'Dorothy, so help me, if you make a scene like that in public again, I won't be responsible for what happens.'

Harvey's jaundiced gaze followed the couple as they made their way out into the hall. 'Neither will I, if she pulls another of her stunts in here,' he grumbled from behind the bar. He grinned suddenly. 'But I guess we needn't worry for a while, Georgi. She'll scoff all the wine you send up and spend the rest of the afternoon sleeping it off.'

'I hope you're right,' replied Georgina with deep feeling.

But Harvey wasn't right.

At five o'clock she was discussing tomorrow's staff meeting with Jill when she heard something that sounded uncomfortably like a rocket screeching. But of course this was October—Hallowe'en firecracker time. She and Jill looked at each other, sighed, and carried on with their conversation.

Five minutes later, Agnes waddled into the office and said glumly, 'I think you'd better come, Georgi. That Mrs Durham is screaming like a banshee upstairs. I got her back in her room, but she keeps howling that her husband has disappeared. She thinks he's drowned himself. If you ask me, he'd be doing us all a favour if he drowned *her*. Thing is, though, she says she's called the police.'

*   *   *

Georgina collapsed into the chair behind her desk and kicked her shoes off. It seemed as if a century had passed since she'd last sat down, but in reality it was only a few hours. She had a feeling she must look as if she'd aged a century too, but at the moment she didn't much care. All she could think of was the insane drama that had just taken place in her hotel.

Mrs Durham, playing the part of panic-stricken wife to its hysterical hilt, had insisted to anyone who would listen that her husband had been so upset by an argument they'd had over a fly she'd found in her gin that he'd walked out of the hotel threatening to do away with himself. She explained, repeatedly, that she hadn't believed him at first, but when he wasn't back three hours later she'd had no choice but to call for the police. She wanted them to drag the lake for his remains.

Inevitably, the police had been followed by a bevy of gleeful reporters. In the midst of the uproar, Mr Durham, smelling discreetly of whisky, had returned to point out that he'd had no intention of ending his life, thank you, but had been obliged to get out of the hotel before he was tempted to end Dorothy's. This husbandly statement had occasioned another round of hysterics from Mrs Durham, official grunts from the police and much enthusiastic scribbling from the reporters.

Georgina had done her best with all of them, at the same time trying to pacify her curious and excited staff, some of whom had done *their* best to add to the confusion and drama. But now, when she was totally drained and exhausted, she had to make a crucial decision.

The story would hit the Washington papers in the morning. Mr Durham was a very public figure, so it would also hit the California papers. If it was a dull day on the news front, possibly even the front page. And

Clayton O'Neill had a reputation for never missing a thing, especially if it concerned his hotels. Which meant that really she had no choice. She must get the story to him first, even though all she felt like doing was lying down on the floor and going to sleep.

'But please, God,' she whispered to her silent office, 'don't make me have to talk to Clayte.'

She picked up the phone. There was no answer from Fred Charlton's office, which was hardly surprising at this hour. She thought for a moment, and then, with great reluctance, and telling herself that Clayte was bound to have left by now too, she asked to be put through to Mr O'Neill. Yes, of course he'd have left, she encouraged herself without much conviction. And in that case all she could do was send him a fax and hope that he read it before he saw the papers in the morning. At least she would have done her best. Clayte had never given her his home address, and his number was bound to be unlisted.

The phone rang six times, and she was about to hang up with relief when a voice barked, 'What? This better be important, Charlton. I'm just about to wind up the Sheridan deal.'

Georgina's powers of speech deserted her. She opened her mouth but only a croak came out.

'What is this?' the voice barked again. 'I haven't got time to play games.'

'I—it's not a game,' she managed to whisper. 'And I'm not Charlton.'

There was a long silence on the other end of the line, then finally Clayte said in a tone that reminded her of winter ice breaking on the lake, 'I thought we agreed that Charlton would handle any business connected with Snowlake.'

She closed her eyes. This was a thousand times more painful than she'd imagined, but somehow she had to get through it. 'Charlton's left. I didn't think the business would wait.'

'Georgina——' His voice sharpened. 'Has something happened? You sound——'

'Tired?' said Georgina. 'Yes, I am. And, yes, something has happened.'

Stumbling over her words a little, and trying desperately to sound as calm and controlled as she had been forced to remain all evening, Georgina explained the events leading up to her phone call. 'I thought you ought to know at once,' she finished. 'In case the Press——'

'Yes,' he snapped. 'Quite right.'

That seemed to be it then. Again she was about to hang up when Clayte added much less abruptly, 'Georgina, are you all right?'

'Yes, of course I am,' she lied.

'You don't sound it.'

'Oh. Well, it's all been a bit exhausting, and I'm not used to vanishing guests and melodrama in the upstairs hallway.' She knew the words sounded flippant. She hadn't meant them to really, but that was the way they'd come out. Probably she was more exhausted than she'd thought.

'I think that's all I can tell you,' she finished, hoping she sounded cool and composed. 'If there are any further developments, I'll contact Charlton.'

'Georgina...'

But Georgina had had all she could take. A huge effort of will had enabled her to survive the conversation thus far, and to listen to Clayte's beloved voice without dissolving into uncontrollable tears. But she couldn't hold on a moment longer.

She took a deep breath and put the receiver down without giving him a chance to finish his sentence. After that she laid her arms on the desk, laid her head on them, and allowed the tears to flow unimpeded. By the time they finally dried, she was asleep.

Somewhere in the hotel a phone was ringing. Then it became a woman's muffled sobs. Her own perhaps? Georgina stared at the file tray on her desk, and suddenly it wasn't a file tray any more, but Dorothy Durham's open mouth. She gave a low moan and tried to push it away, but as soon as she moved her head hit the corner of something sharp—her desk pen set. She blinked. What was happening to her? None of this was real, so she must be dreaming. But why was she sleeping in the hotel? And why was her pillow so hard?

She gave another moan, louder this time, and as she struggled to sit up she heard a man's deep baritone exclaiming, 'My God, Georgina! What the hell . . . ?'

The next thing she knew she was being carried up the stairs in Clayte's arms. He was wearing a severe dark grey suit and a maroon tie, and he smelled of soft leather and spice. But Clayte was in Los Angeles, so obviously she was still dreaming—and if that was the case she didn't much want to wake up.

When she did, she found she was lying in one of the Inn's king-sized beds clad only in her sensible white slip. The curtains were drawn, but she could see afternoon sunlight filtering through the chink where they came together. Beside her on the bed a dark shape lay breathing steadily...

She gasped and sat up. The shape moved too and extended a nicely muscled arm.

'Lie down, Georgina,' said Clayte. 'Even if you were up to it I wouldn't have any plans to seduce you.'

CHAPTER NINE

GEORGINA brushed a hand over her eyes. She wasn't dreaming now, she was sure of it. But in that case what was she doing in Clayte's bed? For that matter, what was Clayte doing in Snowlake? And why didn't he have any plans to seduce her if he'd taken so much trouble to get her this far? She was conscious of a vague sense of disappointment, and then of a sharp pain in her head. He'd said something about her not being up to it...

Oh. Oh, dear lord. All at once the events of...was it yesterday?...came flooding back. Mrs Durham's hysterics, the police, the reporters, the phone call to Clayte, the tears—and in the end she'd fallen asleep at her desk.

'Lie down, Georgina.' Clayte's firm voice interrupted her confused and unhappy memories. 'You look as if you could do with a good tune-up.'

Georgina gasped, then felt a totally unexpected urge to giggle. It had been such a long time since she'd been in any mood to laugh—and she supposed it wasn't really appropriate now. Waking up after a management crisis in the bed of a man who had admitted quite frankly that she wasn't his idea of the ideal woman was not funny. Nothing that had happened to her recently was funny.

Clayte put his hands on her shoulders and pulled her back down beside him. 'I told you to lie down,' he said softly.

'I know.' She gave up trying to react as she knew she ought to, and permitted herself a half-hearted chuckle. 'But I think you mistook me for your car.'

He reached for the bedside lamp, propped himself up on one elbow and gazed down at her, and she saw that he didn't appear to be wearing any clothes. 'Not likely,' he said, appraising her very thoroughly from the waist up. 'My car generally does exactly what I tell it. And I keep it in excellent shape, which is more than can be said for you at the moment.'

'Thanks,' said Georgina. 'Clayte, what am I doing here?'

'Nothing. More's the pity.'

'All right, what are *you* doing here?'

'See answer Number One.'

'Clayte!' She put a hand over her face because the gentle seduction in his eyes made her want to do all sorts of things she was sure would be better left undone.

'Yes?' he replied innocently.

'Clayte, please—don't.' She peered at him through her fingers. 'It doesn't seem right when you're—you're...'

'When I'm what?'

'Going out with Vicki Romero.'

'Who told you that? She spent a night in one of my hotels once, but that hardly qualifies as "going out". The child's hardly out of diapers, for Pete's sake.'

'Oh.' Georgina heard the reproving note in his voice, and couldn't think of anything else to say. The Inn's unreliable grapevine had struck again. 'Why am I in your bed?' she asked finally. 'What's happened?'

'Absolutely nothing has happened, as I've already told you. And I wish you'd stop harping on that point. You are in my bed strictly because you passed out on me— overwork and exhaustion, I imagine—and I didn't want to leave you alone.'

'Oh.' Georgina lowered her hand cautiously. Clayte was lying on his back again, staring up at the ceiling with one arm looped behind his head. 'I suppose it didn't occur to you that you could quite well keep an eye on me with your clothes on?'

'Watch it, Mrs Kettrick. I've had better days than this one myself, and your situation at the moment is precarious. In fact I'd say I've got the upper hand—which I could very easily be persuaded to use.'

'No, you couldn't,' said Georgina confidently. 'You said I'm not up to it, remember.'

'Yes, but at that point I was talking about seduction.'

'Well, I'm talking about clothes,' she replied, beginning to wonder if she was losing her mind. This whole conversation, along with her unlikely position, had an air of unreality about it. She turned her head away, because the sight of his tough body lying so close to her own was not at all conducive to rational thought. At once her mind seemed to clear, and it came to her that clothes were not the issue. The issue was that by now it was more than probable that the entire staff was aware that she was in bed with the Inn's owner—which would be bad enough if she and Clayte were actually engaged in the activity they'd be assumed to be enjoying. Even more of a waste of her reputation if they were not.

The place where she had hit her head on the pen set began to throb.

'Clayte,' she asked, 'who's looking after the Inn? It's afternoon, isn't it? Everyone must know——'

'Georgina, you have a perfectly capable staff,' he interrupted with a touch of impatience. 'If they weren't, they wouldn't be working for me. So I presume they can manage on their own for a couple of hours.'

'Yes, I suppose they can, but...' Georgina gathered her thoughts together and went on quickly. 'But if they know we're here they're bound to think we're in bed——'

'We are in bed. Does it matter? As far as I know, I have a right to do what I like in my own hotel. Besides, I told Jill the truth—that I'd been travelling all night and intended to catch up on my sleep. I also pointed out that you'd had a rough night and needed the rest.'

'Yes, but—Clayte, they must know we're in the same room.'

'I expect they do,' he said indifferently. 'Is that a problem?'

Georgina was silent. She supposed it wasn't really a problem except in her own mind. The staff liked her, and Agnes, for one, had even informed her outright that it was time she had a man in her life. All the same, the situation was awkward. In more ways than one, she thought miserably, because her uninvited bedmate would soon depart again, leaving her more unsettled, bereft and lonely than she'd been before.

'I thought,' she said carefully, 'that you said it was bad policy to——'

'To make love to my managers?' He put a hand on her cheek and made her face him. 'I know, but sometimes circumstances change.'

Yes, when it happens to suit you, she thought bitterly. There was an enigmatic light in his eyes that she hadn't seen there before, but she supposed all it meant was that he'd decided the circumstances were ripe for seduction. She edged away from him, and put a foot over the edge of the bed.

At once his arm clamped her around her waist so that she couldn't get up. 'You're not going anywhere,' he said, smiling implacably.

Georgina began to think he was right, because he was stroking his hand over her hip and down her leg, then lifting the plain white slip to tantalise the inside of her thigh. 'You said I wasn't——' She gasped as automatically her body started to respond.

'Up to it?' His eyes were compelling and hypnotic, like dark crystals in which she couldn't see the future. 'Yes, but I was wrong about that, wasn't I? You need more than soothing platitudes to make you whole.'

She nodded dumbly, because now his hand was on her stomach, and she could feel his long leg easing gently between her thighs. Oh, he was definitely right about that. She did need more than platitudes to soothe her. She needed love and reassurance and hope. And she knew that whatever the consequences, however much she might regret her capitulation later, the only thing that mattered at this moment was that Clayte was here, caring for her, and that he wanted her as much as she wanted him.

With a little sigh she gathered him into her arms. Clayte groaned, and as she began to trail her nails lightly down his back he closed his mouth possessively over hers.

After that there was only the heady delirium of rediscovering the passion they had shared so beautifully on the pink plush rug two weeks before. Georgina welcomed him with her heart and with her body, and later, as they lay spent in each other's arms, she felt a sense of completeness that seemed to flood her whole world with bright light. She was at peace now, and no matter what happened in the future she would carry this moment in her heart. Clayte had done that for her, as he had meant to. And she was grateful.

Some time later he disentangled his limbs from hers and sat up. 'You're incredible, my Georgina,' he said softly, running a finger lightly down her nose. 'I've never known a woman who gave so much.'

Georgina closed her eyes quickly. His words brought back the remembrance that he had known other women—women very different from herself. Sophisticated ladies who laughed with him, tumbled into his bed and into his life, and then moved on again without looking back. That was the kind of liaison he'd always chosen.

So, sooner than usual perhaps, he would expect her to move along too.

'You were very satisfactory yourself,' she said to him with a brittle little laugh. No way was she going to let him know just how much he meant to her. She supposed he had come back to Snowlake because of the Durhams—obviously he didn't trust her to handle the publicity on her own. This little side-trip into a hotel bedroom probably hadn't even been part of his plan. It had happened because she needed comfort and the time was right, not because Clayte had in any way changed his mind about her.

'Satisfactory!' He swore softly. 'I'll give you satisfactory, Mrs Kettrick.' He leaned over and pressed his hands into the pillow on either side of her head. Then he lowered his head and kissed her so soundly that when he finally rolled away again her brain felt as if it were swimming round in circles.

Clayte, on the other hand, seemed unmoved. He stood up and vanished into the bathroom. Georgina watched him go, as always fascinated by the almost feral way he walked. He really was a remarkable hunk of a man, she thought dispassionately. She had to be dispassionate, because if she allowed herself to feel she wouldn't be able to do what must be done.

Quickly she slipped out of bed and began to search for her clothes. Her skirt and jacket were laid neatly over an antique oriental chair, looking a lot like a bag-lady's discards. No amount of shaking was likely to remove the creases caused by last night's crisis, which meant that she would have to call Agnes for an iron before she ventured out into the hall.

She was sitting on the edge of the bed staring gloomily into space when Clayte emerged from the bathroom sporting a towel and a wolf-like smile. He looked exactly as he had the day she met him. Swallowing hard, and purposely avoiding his eyes, she dodged around him, slammed the bathroom door, and rested her head against the mirror. It felt cool, a relief from the heat smouldering through her body. On the other side of the door, she thought she heard the telephone ringing.

When Georgina finally gathered the courage to look at her face, she saw that Clayte had meant it when he'd said she was in need of a tune-up. A paint job wouldn't do any harm either, she thought ruefully. Her eyes looked bruised, as if she hadn't slept for weeks, and her complexion was the colour of putty.

She turned on the bath and did her best to soak away the damage. By the time she returned to the bedroom, wrapped in a towel, Clayte was already dressed in his grey suit.

'I'm presenting a businesslike front to the public,' he explained when he saw her staring. His gaze travelled appreciatively over the pale expanse of her skin. 'Which you, at this moment, are not, I'm pleased to say. I have to confess I much prefer you the way you are.'

'If the public is female, I'm sure they'd much prefer you in your bath-towel.' Georgina, disconcerted by the naked admiration in his eyes, spoke without stopping to think.

Clayte smiled meditatively. 'Perhaps, but I'm not much interested in the preferences of women I don't happen to know. However, if *you* prefer the bath-towel...'

'I'd prefer an iron,' said Georgina, who felt at a distinct disadvantage in her towel.

He raised an eyebrow. 'Is that so? And what were you proposing to iron? Me?'

'Why didn't I think of that?' she muttered. 'You could do with some flattening.' At first she wasn't sure why she felt irritated with him. Then she realised it was because once again Clayte had invaded her quiet life, swept her off her feet, and was now preparing to drop her in—in a rosebush probably. It would be appropriate.

'I see that delightful interlude in bed hasn't improved your tongue, Mrs Kettrick,' he observed laconically. 'Obviously I'll have to work on it some more.' He spoke pleasantly enough, yet Georgina had a feeling he meant it. If he did, he was in for a rude awakening.

She shook her head. 'No. I don't think so.'

'Don't you? We'll see. In the meantime, Lori informs me that the lobby is overflowing with reporters. Possibly female ones. I'll deal with them while you get yourself dressed.'

Georgina was still standing in the middle of the floor, blinking at him, when he curved a hand round the back of her neck, kissed her hard, and left the room with a nonchalant wave.

She sat down heavily on the bed, and after a while picked up the phone and asked Agnes to send her up an iron.

'Huh,' snorted Agnes. 'I hoped you had something better to do than ironing.'

Georgina smiled wryly and hung up. Her suspicion that the entire staff knew where she'd been all day had just been most unsubtly confirmed. And it wasn't going to make her life any simpler. Damn Clayte anyway. He could so easily have been a little more discreet.

By the time she started downstairs, Georgina was ready not only to iron him, but to starch him and fold him as well. It was as good a way as any to take her mind off the fact that, inevitably, he would soon be leaving Snowlake again.

She paused with her hand on the banister. That was the whole problem, wasn't it? She loved Clayte so much that the thought of losing him was an agony that no amount of self-delusion could dispel. And she *would* lose him. Of that there was no question. She dug her teeth into her lower lip, and tried to concentrate on that minor pain as she made her way down to the lobby.

'Mr O'Neill, don't you think this whole incident could have been avoided if Mrs Kettrick had handled the matter of the fly in the drink more professionally?' The probing voice of a decidedly female reporter, with red hair, struck Georgina's ears just as she reached the bottom step. She froze where she stood.

'More professionally?' Clayte's cool drawl washed over her like balm on an open wound. 'What, exactly, do you mean by "more professionally"? That she should have ordered a search of all the hotel glasses for concealed flies? Or, in this case, pipe ash? I hardly think that would have helped the situation. In the circumstances, Mrs Kettrick did everything she could. I'm entirely—um— satisfied with her performance.'

Only Georgina noticed his slight emphasis on the 'satisfied'. His eyes rested on her with a proprietorial gleam as she moved up beside him, and she knew that the words weren't nearly as innocuous as they sounded. She dropped her gaze quickly and studied the intricate weave of the deep red carpet at her feet.

Clayte answered several more questions politely and with a certain brisk impatience, and the reporters then turned to Georgina. But when the one who had questioned her handling of the incident asked her if she approved of guests drinking in the bedrooms Clayte interrupted before she had a chance to reply.

'Mrs Kettrick respects the privacy of our guests,' he said firmly. 'And now, if you don't mind, this has been a very taxing experience for her and I believe it's time she had something to eat. I'm afraid you'll have to excuse us.'

The reporters' collective mouths fell open as Clayte took Georgina's arm and began to propel her across the lobby and through the door.

'One more question, Mr O'Neill,' shouted the persistent redhaired inquisitor. 'Is there any truth to the rumour that you and Mrs Kettrick are involved on a personal level?'

Clayte stopped, turned round, and replied evenly, 'It's none of your damn business, is it? Any more impertinent questions?'

There weren't, but by the time they got outside Georgina's face had turned an interesting shade of poppy-pink. 'Clayte,' she said despairingly, 'you shouldn't have said that. Now they'll all think we *are* involved.'

'Then they'll be right for once, won't they?'

'Not for...' She wanted to say not for long. But the words choked her, and all of a sudden she felt that she just couldn't bear it any longer. Being with Clayte again, watching him move, feeling his hand on her arm and listening to his low, caressing voice—it all became a deep, painful ache. Whatever the consequences, for now she had to get away.

Clayte was making for the hotel's sedan again, and when he released her arm to pull his keys out of his pocket Georgina seized the opportunity to run. Without a word she turned tail and bolted for her own small Mazda, which was parked on the other side of the car park.

'Georgina! What the hell...?' The sound of Clayte's angry roar was drowned out by the raised voices of a gaggle of clamouring reporters who, discovering that their quarry was still within striking distance, were tumbling across the asphalt in hot pursuit.

When Georgina glanced over her shoulder, she saw that Clayte was totally surrounded, so she put on a spurt and tugged open the door of her car. It took him several seconds to extricate himself from the persistent throng, and by that time she was already on the road. After a while she looked in the rear-view mirror, half expecting to see the sedan behind her. But the road was empty.

By the time she got home it was raining. Wearily she pushed open the door and kicked her shoes off. Tea, she thought, dragging herself into the kitchen. Hot black tea with lemon. Maybe that would help to melt the chill that seemed to have crept deep into her bones.

She wondered vaguely what had come over her. Why she was here, making tea, instead of with Clayte, making love. Some instinct of self-preservation, she supposed. An instinct which told her that the more time she spent with him, the deeper the scars his memory would leave on her heart.

Rain was streaking drearily down the window as she carried her tea to the table and sat down. Clayte hadn't followed her, so he must have taken her abrupt departure as a signal that their brief affair was over. Short of another Durham crisis—which God forbid!—he wouldn't be back.

Now, once again, she would have to glue together the remnants of her life. Perhaps, eventually, the wounds would heal to the point where they didn't show much. And maybe one day there might even come a time when they didn't hurt. She took a long gulp of tea and wished she could truly believe that day would come.

Some time later, as she gazed dully into her empty cup and listened to the sound of the rain, Georgina thought she heard a knock on the door. Then she realised that the wind had risen while she'd been staring bleakly into the future. It was only a rose branch tapping on the window.

The sound came again, and this time it was no tap, but a steady pounding. Reluctantly she got up to investigate.

When she turned on the porch light and peered through the peephole, she saw that Clayte was standing on the doorstep holding a bouquet of yellow roses. In spite of the flowers, he looked unyielding, hard-bitten, and more like a pirate than ever. A fierce, bloodthirsty pirate bent on plunder and pillage. For a moment Georgina had the ridiculous sensation that if she opened the door to him she might very well end up walking the plank.

She stared at him for a long time, drinking in the tautly held body, the deep-set eyes that she had seen express gentleness as well as anger, and the sensual lips twisting in something that was either pain or frustration. Then, with a full heart, she turned and walked back to the kitchen.

'Georgina! I know you're there.' Clayte's bellow carried over the wind to the back of the cottage. 'And if you don't have this door open in ten seconds I'll have it broken down in five. One—two...'

Georgina stood up and made her way back to the peephole. 'Five—six...'

Oh, God, he meant it. He was laying the roses in a flowerbox and taking off his jacket.

'Clayte,' she shouted at him. 'Please go away.'

He ignored her and proceeded to roll up his shirt-sleeves.

'Clayte,' she tried again desperately. 'Leave me alone.'

He flexed his forearm and glanced towards the sound of her voice. 'Seven—eight ... Are you going to open this door, Georgina?'

'No.'

'Right.' He put his shoulder against the white-painted panelling. 'Then you can take my word for it that by the time I'm through with you you'll wish you had.'

Yes, that sounded like Clayte. He was used to getting what he wanted. When he didn't, the person who stood in his way could expect to pay for it. She wondered what form his penalty would take, and was puzzled to find that she didn't really care. Nothing seemed to matter much any more.

'Are you threatening me?' she asked tiredly.

'Very definitely. Nine...'

Her eyes widened as she saw him step back and bunch his left shoulder. When he said, 'Ten,' and began to run at the door, she pulled it open.

Georgina didn't move fast enough, and Clayte, unable to halt his own momentum, hurtled through the opening and struck her left side with the full force of an athletic two hundred pounds.

She gasped, he grunted, and both of them fell to the floor.

Clayte recovered first. 'Georgina, are you all right?' His voice grated with concern.

'Not particularly,' she said. 'I am bruised, winded, and I ache all over.'

He propped himself on his elbow and stared down at her, his gaze travelling intently over each one of her spread-eagled limbs. Then, when he was apparently satisfied that her condition wasn't terminal, he said, 'Serves you right. Why didn't you move out of the way?'

'Because I wasn't expecting to be knocked down by a hulking great tiger on the rampage.'

'Thank you. And why not? I told you you'd regret it if you didn't open up.'

'I did open up. That was my big mistake.'

'No, Mrs Kettrick, your big mistake was running out on me. *My* big mistake was letting you.'

Georgina gazed up at the face hovering above her. The face of the man she adored. He didn't look angry any more, he looked tired, and in his eyes there was an expression of such deep tenderness that her heart turned over. Was it—could it be for her? She didn't quite believe it, but hope welled up none the less.

'Clayte,' she said cautiously. 'You didn't exactly let me. But why—well, why should you care?'

'That,' he said, reaching for her and pulling her hard against his chest, 'is just about the dumbest question you've ever asked me.'

'It's not...' She stopped as a shadow fell across the open doorway and a gust of wind flapped at her clothes.

'Oh. Sorry...' Gordon's embarrassed voice trailed off in a violent clearing of the throat. Georgina broke away from Clayte's embrace and sat up as if she were a puppet on the end of a string. Awkwardly, she began to smooth down her skirt.

'Hello, Gordon,' she said. 'Would you like to come in?'

'Er—no.' Her ex sounded as if he were being strangled. 'Heard shouting. Isabel said... well, anyway—um—worried about you.'

'No need to be,' said Clayte brusquely, as he stood up and began to brush off his shirt. 'I'm looking after Georgina.'

'Mmm, saw that. Georgina, is he—are you...?'

'Yes,' said Georgina. 'I'm just fine.' She looked up at Clayte, who was standing above her with his dark gaze fixed disparagingly on Gordon, and somehow, against all the odds, she knew it was true. She was more than fine.

Gordon nodded, grunted something about that being all right, then, and shot off down the path like a rabbit escaping from a snake.

Clayte shut the door and held out his hand. Georgina took it, and he pulled her up beside him. For a few seconds they stood still, staring blankly into each other's startled eyes. Then Clayte's lips quirked, and Georgina's shoulders began to shake uncontrollably. When he held out his arms, she fell into them.

CHAPTER TEN

'POOR Gordon,' said Georgina guiltily, dabbing the back of her hand at the tears of laughter streaming down her cheeks. 'He looked so—so——'

'Stupid?' suggested Clayte, who had never troubled to conceal his contempt for her well-meaning ex. 'I never could understand what you saw in him.'

Georgina felt herself bristling. Gordon had, after all, been trying to help.

'He was kind,' she said, not laughing any more. 'Irresponsible in the old days, but kind. He still is.' She pulled away from Clayte and went to stare out of the window.

'And I'm not, I suppose.' He came up behind her and dropped his hands over her hips.

Georgina felt her mouth go dry, whether because of the hands, or because his tone was an outright rebuke, she wasn't sure.

'You can be,' she admitted. 'Provided you get everything your own way.'

'Which I usually do,' he pointed out.

'Yes, I guess that's true. Most of the time. It's very bad for you.'

'Is it?' he asked. 'Does that mean I'm not going to get what I want this time?'

'I don't know,' she replied, jabbing a finger at a speck of dust on the sill. 'But then I don't know what you want, do I? I'm not sure I ever have.'

Clayte's grip on her hips tightened, and he turned her very firmly to face him. When she looked up, she noticed for the first time that his white shirt was damp from the rain. It clung to his broad chest like a silk skin.

'Your jacket,' she said. 'You left it outside.'

He gave an exclamation of annoyance and released her. 'So I did. Wait here.'

Well, where else did he think she could go? Georgina wondered. Was he so in the habit of giving orders that he gave them without even thinking?

'I'm waiting,' she replied with an acidity that appeared to be lost on him as he strode to the door, jerked it open, and retrieved his jacket and a bouquet of rain-spattered roses.

He threw the wet jacket on to her flowered love-seat, making her wince, and held out the roses. 'These are for you,' he said.

She accepted them. 'What are the flowers about?' she asked suspiciously as she went into the kitchen to find a vase.

He didn't answer, so when she returned to the living-room she said, 'Thank you. Are you making amends again? If so, there was really no need.'

To her surprise, he scowled as if she'd slapped him in the face—which, come to think of it, she'd been tempted to do on a number of occasions. 'Wasn't there?' he asked.

She frowned at him, puzzled. 'I don't think so. What do you mean?'

'You ran off on me, didn't you? I presume I brought it on myself, although I have to admit I've no idea how. Incidentally, I didn't like it.'

'I don't think you were meant to,' said Georgina, who at this moment, with Clayte's damp body looming over her, couldn't quite remember what had made her run away in the first place.

'That's what I figured.' With an abruptness that startled her, he swung around and flung himself into a chair. 'OK,' he said, holding out his arms. 'Make it up to me.'

Georgina blinked at him, unable to account for his abrupt change of mood. She found her eyes riveted by the wet stretch of shirt across his chest. 'I don't think——' she began.

He grinned. 'No need to. Just do as you're told.'

She licked her lips, and took a doubtful step towards him. Then, before she realised what he was up to, he had grabbed her wrist and pulled her on to his knees. 'Right,' he said, placing both hands on her waist. 'Kiss me.'

Mesmerised, Georgina bent forward and touched her lips to his mouth.

'Not good enough,' he said, shaking his head. 'Never mind, there'll be time to work on it later. Now, tell me what you meant by running away.'

Georgina couldn't seem to concentrate. The feel of his thighs underneath her, his wicked black eyes and the strong hands holding her waist, were all conspiring to take her mind off practical considerations—like the fact that Clayte would soon be leaving her for good.

She returned to reality with a jolt. 'I decided,' she told him steadily, 'that since you'd be going soon there really wasn't any point in prolonging the agony.'

The change in his expression was dramatic. One minute he was raising questioning black eyebrows, confidently demanding an answer—the next he looked as if she'd stabbed him to the heart. 'Agony?' he repeated. 'Georgina—was it that bad?'

She closed her eyes. Why lie to him? Pride wasn't worth a penny compared to the bittersweet pleasure of telling him the truth she suspected he had known and disdained from the beginning. 'Yes,' she said. 'It was that bad. Worse.'

'Why?' He lifted a hand to cup it around her cheek. 'Georgina, please look at me.'

Georgina looked at him, and he was gazing at her with so much guilt, and so much yearning, that she said simply, 'Because I love you, of course.'

At once thick lashes swept down to shield his eyes, but his grip on her waist tightened, and when he said in a voice so choked with feeling that she could scarcely make out the words, 'Thank you, my darling, it's a whole lot more than I deserve,' she buried her face in his neck and gave way to long-withheld tears.

Clayte patted her shoulder with awkward tenderness. 'For God's sake, don't cry,' he muttered. 'I never meant to make you cry.'

Georgina sniffed, gulped and finally managed to stem the flow. 'I'm sorry,' she murmured. 'I—it's just that I thought you'd be angry.'

'Angry? Why should I be angry?'

'Because—because I said I love you.'

'Georgina. My dear, beautiful, totally ridiculous Georgina...' He paused and lifted her chin so that she was looking straight into his eyes. 'Don't you know those are the three words I've been longing to hear—the words I was profoundly afraid you'd never speak? My darling girl, when I walked out on you, deliberately rejecting everything you had to offer, I knew there was a damned good chance I was killing whatever feeling you might have for me. And I thought that was best. For you.' He rubbed a thumb across her cheek, gently wiping away a tear.

Georgina sucked in her breath, hoping, but still not quite daring to believe. 'But I thought—I don't understand. Why should you want me to love you when I'm exactly the sort of woman you've always avoided? And anyway, I was sure—sure that you knew—that the reason you thought of firing me and then decided I could deal entirely through Fred Charlton was—well, because you didn't want some lovesick albatross hanging on your neck.'

Clayte dropped her chin abruptly. 'Lovesick albatross?' he repeated in a suffocated voice. 'Is that what you are?'

She gave him a small, doubtful smile. 'Lovesick anyway,' she admitted. 'I thought albatross went with the territory.'

'Oh, my love.' Clayte wrapped both his arms around her and pulled her head on to his shoulder. 'It's my own fault, of course,' he muttered half to himself, as he raked his fingers gently through her curls. 'And you're quite right. I did guess that you loved me. It's exactly why I had to get away. Because I suspected I was beginning to love you too. Aunt Josephine knew it the moment I came back from firing Steve Novak.'

'Your Aunt Josephine is a very perceptive lady,' Georgina murmured into his neck. She still couldn't quite understand what Clayte was telling her, but the rain had stopped outside and somewhere above her head a grey cloud seemed to be lifting, turning into bright sunshine that made her want to sing.

'Mmm. She is also a very bossy, persistent and opinionated lady. She told me if I didn't have the sense to marry you she would have to move into my penthouse and take me over herself. She's not above a bit of terrorism when it suits her.'

'Oh,' said Georgina, digesting this startling information. 'So—um—did you let her move in?'

'No. But I wouldn't have been able to hold her back for long. Aunt Josephine in tank formation is America's most underrated weapon.'

Georgina choked into his shoulder. 'That's all very well,' she sputtered, 'but——'

'I know,' he said. 'We're not married, are we? The threat of Aunt Josephine still looms.'

Georgina stopped sputtering as a startling knot formed in her intestines. What did Clayte mean by that? That they were never going to be married? Oh, he wanted her to love him, she had no doubt about that. But he'd said nothing about a permanent arrangement.

She couldn't seem to breathe, and suddenly she had to get up. Clayte's intoxicating touch and the warm, male scent of his skin were clouding her brain. As his fingers stroked gently down her back, she put a hand on the arm of the chair and pushed herself on to her feet. By the time he realised she wasn't just changing her position, she was on her way out to the kitchen.

She reached for the tap, intending to splash water on her face, but at once she felt a firm hand close over her wrist. Then she found herself hauled summarily back to the living-room.

'And where did you think you were going?' Clayte asked with surprising equanimity.

'Away from you,' she said. There was no point in dissembling.

Clayte wiped a hand across his face, and when he lowered it his expression had changed from questioning amiability to deadpan inscrutability. 'I see,' he said. 'I was right, then.'

'Right? What do you mean?'

'That loving me isn't enough.' He turned his back on her and went to stand by the mantel, his movements so stiff with tension that Georgina wanted to fling her arms around him and hold him to her until she had stroked away all the tell-tale signs of strain. But she forced herself to remain where she was.

'Clayte,' she began quietly, 'I don't see——'

'No,' he interrupted harshly. 'Why should you?'

She stared at his dark bowed head, longing to touch him, but certain that he would only push her away if she did. 'Perhaps if you'd explain, tell me what it is you want,' she suggested.

'All right.' He didn't turn round, but spoke in a low, flat voice to the brick fireplace. 'When I left you the last time, it was because I was certain we were wrong for each other. You wanted all the things I hated—and how could I possibly make you happy when I'd have to uproot you from everything you'd worked to achieve?' He gestured blindly at the room behind him, with its bright paint and pretty furnishings. 'The home you'd never had until you came to Snowlake—the friends— even the roses.' He put an elbow on the mantel and pounded his forehead with his fist. 'And I *was* right, wasn't I? I'm asking too much. You're not willing to leave all this for me.'

'Clayte,' said Georgina, who suddenly understood what was meant by the expression 'heart in mouth', 'Clayte, do you mean...? You're not...? I mean, you couldn't be asking me...? That is...'

'Damn it, woman,' roared Clayte, losing patience and spinning round to advance across the room in two strides. 'Yes, I'm asking you to marry me, God help me. It's probably the stupidest thing I've ever asked, and I deserve exactly the answer I know I'm going to get. But I love you, Georgina Kettrick, and I don't want you to be called by that idiot next door's name any more.' He stopped just six inches from her nose and stood over her with both fists clenched at his sides. He was scowling, his jaw was thrust out, and he looked as though he was spoiling for a fight. But to Georgina that belligerent face was the dearest face in her whole world.

She put a hand on his still damp chest. 'My name used to be Darling,' she said softly.

He stared at her, his deep eyes expressing a desperate vulnerability. Georgina, biting back a sob, took pity on him and lifted her hands to his face. 'But I'd be very happy to change it to O'Neill,' she assured him with a watery smile.

For several seconds Clayte said nothing. He just looked at her as if she'd offered him a trip to the moon. Then he exhaled a very long breath and pulled her into his arms. 'My dear, beautiful Georgina,' he whispered into her ear, 'don't you know you'll always be Darling to me?'

It was some time later when Georgina raised her head from Clayte's chest as they sat peacefully entwined on the sofa, and asked hesitantly, 'Clayte, did you actually *mean* to ask me to marry you?'

Clayte shifted his body to get a better look at her. 'Are you out of your mind?' he asked curiously. 'Or are you under the impression that I am?'

'No, of course not——'

'Then what on earth makes you think I go round proposing to people by mistake?'

Georgina shook her head. 'No, I mean when you first came back. I thought you came because of the Durhams—that you didn't trust me to handle the Press on my own.'

'Of course I trusted you. But after making life hell for myself and everyone near me for weeks I was coming round to the idea that *you* might have something to do with my bad temper. Even without Aunt Josephine's daily reminders I knew that sooner or later I'd have to give us a chance. Then you phoned, and when I heard your voice again—you sounded so alone and exhausted and yet so brave—I knew I couldn't wait any longer. But you hung up on me, which left me very doubtful of my reception.' He traced a finger gently along the line of her lips and smiled wryly.

'I see,' said Georgina. 'So you solved the problem by trapping me in your bed and ruining my reputation with the staff.'

He grinned unrepentently. 'The opportunity was too good to miss. Besides, it worked, didn't it?'

'What did?'

'You accepted me. Thereby saving your saintly reputation. Which, by the way, is undeserved. You kiss much too efficiently to be a saint.'

'Do I?' said Georgina dreamily. 'I do other unsaintly things quite well too.'

Clayte made a face. 'I know. You cook apple pies, which are definitely an invention of the devil.'

Georgina, feeling as if she'd just been hit in the stomach by a football, sat up straight and moved to the other end of the sofa. 'Clayte,' she said, 'I thought— do you mean you still hate—well, all the things I enjoy? Are you really going to lose your temper every time I put on an apron? Because if you are——' She stopped, unable to finish.

Because if he was, as much as she loved him, she wasn't sure she could go through with this marriage. Being Clayte's wife was one thing. But being a jet-set party-girl for him was quite another.

She saw at once that Clayte was aware of how much hung on his answer, because instead of shrugging off her question with a teasing quip he frowned and said, 'Georgina, you and I have to talk.'

Georgina nodded. 'I agree.'

Clayte leaned forward, resting his arms on his knees, and she could see that he found it difficult to speak.

'You know, of course, that my mother died two years ago.'

'Yes. Your aunt Josephine told me. I'm sorry.'

He shook his head impatiently. 'No, it's all right. She went peacefully. But you see—I've never been able to tell you just what my life with her was like. The truth, I suppose, is that I'd greatly prefer to forget it.'

Georgina frowned. 'Was it so bad, then? Aunt Josephine did tell me your mother was very particular about her house, but...'

He gave a bark of laughter so bitter that, although she longed to take him in her arms, she knew he would fling her away if she tried. 'What an understatement. My mother wasn't particular, she was fanatical. Oh, she meant well, of course, but she couldn't conceive of a life that didn't revolve around the stove, the sewing machine, and a cupboard full of polish and soap. I don't know what made her that way, but her perfect home was the most important thing in her life. She didn't know how to talk about anything else. All our conversations were one-way. "Take your feet off that chair. Sit down, you might spill milk on the carpet. Don't touch the curtains. Wash your hands. You're late, and the meal I've worked so hard on is going to spoil. Clayton O'Neill, do you realise you have grass stains on your jeans...?"' He stopped suddenly and buried his face in his hands. 'I'm sorry. I didn't mean to sound like the self-centred little boy I must have been.'

'All children are self-centred,' said Georgina gently.

'Yes. Well, anyway...' He sat up and pushed his hands through his hair. When he turned to face her Georgina thought she saw traces of the unhappy, rebellious little boy who had turned into the hard-headed yet surprisingly tender man she loved. That child was still there in the obstinate set of his mouth and the way his eyes dared her to pity him.

'The point,' he finished grimly, 'is that in the end it was her obsession with the house that drove my father away. He was offered a promotion in another city, and my mother knew that if she went with him we'd have to live in a rented apartment until we could afford another house. She couldn't face that. Not when she'd already found perfection. They discussed it endlessly. I heard them arguing way into the night. In the end, of course, Dad went without her.' The muscles in Clayte's jaw contracted suddenly. 'After that I was the only one around to make a mess, so every spot and stain was laid at my door—usually with cause.'

'You mean your father never came back? Oh, Clayte...'

'Sure he came back. At first. And then he met my aunt Josephine. Would you believe the happiest days of my childhood were spent with those two? They were totally unalike, but it didn't matter.' His voice roughened. 'It wasn't until I'd spent a couple of holidays in their cluttered bungalow that I came to realise all the evil in the world doesn't stem from fingermarks on the wall.'

'Poor Clayte,' said Georgina, touching a hand to his arm.

He shook it off. 'Don't worry. I gave as good as I got. I didn't make my mother's life easy.'

'So your aunt told me,' said Georgina drily.

'Mmm. She would. Aunt Josephine tried to make me see that Mother couldn't help it, that she was insecure and unhappy in spite of all my father's efforts to please her. And she was right, of course.'

'Yes. But I think what you're trying to tell me is that your upbringing has left you with scars—in the form of a permanent horror of domesticity. Clayte, I do understand, but——'

'But you're not about to change to suit me.'

His dark eyes blazed at her with so much passion that she wanted to cry out, Of course I'll change. I love you and nothing else matters. But she couldn't do it, because she knew it wasn't true.

Clayte knew it too. 'It's all right, my love,' he said quietly, his deep voice stroking away her fears. 'You, with your strength and independence, have taught me what I should have understood from the first—that you cook and sew and clean simply because you enjoy it, not as some kind of pathetic security blanket because you're afraid to venture out into the big wide world. You've seen the world, and discovered the value of roots, but that doesn't mean you're afraid of living——'

Georgina shook her head and interrupted. 'No, it doesn't,' she agreed. 'But what about you, Clayte? Are *you* still afraid of apple pies?'

He frowned. 'You haven't been listening to me, have you? I . . .' He stopped, took a long breath, then reached over to take her by the wrist. 'No,' he said roughly. 'The only thing I'm afraid of is losing you. When you ran away from me in the parking lot tonight, I thought I had.'

'But—but you didn't come after me.' Georgina stared at him, half aggrieved, half puzzled. 'Why didn't you?'

He gave her a slow, stomach-curling smile and moved his hand up her arm. 'Roses. I stopped for yellow roses. I wasn't sure a kiss would be enough.'

Georgina's lips parted in anticipation as, gently but with resolution, he began to pull her along the sofa towards him.

As it turned out, a kiss was not enough. Over an hour had passed by the time Georgina, rosy and glowing from love, and once again dressed in her green dressing-gown, floated out to the kitchen to make supper. She told Clayte, who was grinning up at her from the pink plush rug, that as love was now very nicely requited, thank

you, there was no reason for either of them to stop
eating.

Clayte, wearing only his trousers, wandered in after
her. 'There is just one small matter we haven't cleared
up,' he said, running a finger down her spine and making
her gasp.

'What's that?' asked Georgina. She opened the fridge
and removed four large brown eggs.

'Well, we've agreed that I won't beat you up if I see
you wearing an apron. But we haven't agreed that you
won't dig your charming toes in and insist on staying on
in this town. I want to hire a replacement for you, my
love. I need a wife more than I need a manager for
Snowlake.'

Georgina laid the eggs down carefully and turned to
link her arms around his neck. 'Clayte,' she said, smiling
softly into his eyes, 'don't you understand that my home
will always be wherever you are? That you're all the security I'll ever need? I've known it since the night of the
burglary, I think, even though I didn't accept it.'

For answer, Clayte put his arms round her waist and
buried his face in her hair. 'My darling Georgina,' he
murmured.

They stood like that for some time, and then Georgina
muttered something about vegetables. Clayte released
her and watched as she gathered up the makings for a
salad. 'We'll keep your cottage for holidays, of course,'
he said as though she had no say in the matter. 'Our
children will love it as much as you do. And I'll sell my
penthouse and build you the home of your dreams—
somewhere in the hills, but not too far from my office.'

'Will it have roses?' asked Georgina, whose eyes had
mysteriously misted over.

'It will have roses every day of the year. And at night, when I hold you in my arms, their perfume will drift through our dreams.'

'Oh, Clayte. I didn't think you knew how to say things like that.'

Clayte laughed, a little self-consciously. 'To tell you the truth, neither did I.'

Georgina put down a vicious-looking knife, took his face in her hands, and kissed him very tenderly on the lips.

Later, as she busied herself with the eggs while Clayte perched on the edge of the kitchen table, she remembered something else he'd said. 'Do you *like* children?' she asked doubtfully. 'You've never said so before.'

'I don't know,' he admitted with disconcerting honesty. 'I've never had much to do with them. But as long as they're yours I'll love them. Besides, I have a feeling they go with apple pies and aprons.'

Georgina nodded. 'They do. Which reminds me...' She opened the fridge again and pulled out a round, covered dish.

'What's that?' asked Clayte.

She gave him a small, implacable smile and replied casually, 'Apple pie. I just have to heat it in the oven.'

Clayte swallowed—she could see his throat working—and muttered a word she didn't quite catch. After that he said nothing.

But when she removed the pie from the oven at the end of the meal and presented him with a generous portion he gave her a tip-tilted grin, heaved a martyred sigh and picked up his fork with the air of a man stepping bravely out on to the scaffold.

'Clayte?' Georgina frowned across the table at her recently acquired fiancé. 'Why are you making those extraordinary faces? There was nothing wrong with that pie.'

'No,' he said, turning away so that she could only see his profile. 'I'm sure there wasn't.'

Georgina's frown deepened. Didn't he *know* there was nothing wrong with her pie? She bent forward to look at him more closely, and noticed that his seductive lips seemed a little fuller than usual, and that he was rubbing a thumb surreptitiously down the side of his leg. 'Are you practising for Hallowe'en?' she asked sharply.

'What?' He glanced at her briefly and put a hand up to his mouth.

'I said are you practising for Hallowe'en? You seem to be masquerading as an ape. With a bad case of fleas,' she added, as he started to massage his elbow.

Clayte stood up and stalked out of the room. She supposed he was making a dignified exit. Unfortunately the illusion was shattered when she saw his fingers scratch discreetly up his thigh.

Georgina began to clear the table, and when Clayte returned she didn't trouble to look up at once. When she did, she was so startled by his appearance that the remains of the pie almost ended up face down on the floor.

'You've gone all pink and funny-looking,' she gasped.

'I have not,' said Clayte through his teeth, 'gone *pink*. For your information, I've gone a perfectly healthy fire-engine red.'

'But why?' asked Georgina, wiping her hands on a towel. 'What's the matter with you?'

'Do you have any milk?' he demanded, angling his eyes sideways as he deliberately avoided her question.

'Milk?' she repeated. 'You want *milk*?' Whisky, beer, even coffee, she could have accepted. But surely Clayte wasn't the sort of man who drank milk.

'That's what I said. Please,' he added, grudgingly, sitting down at the table and shifting his shoulders uncomfortably against the high back of the chair.

Georgina filled a glass and handed it to him. He swallowed it quickly, ran the back of his hand across his mouth and muttered, 'Thanks. That helps.'

'Helps what?' asked Georgina, now thoroughly annoyed. 'What *is* the matter with you, Clayte?'

'Nothing much,' he replied. She glared at him, and after a pause he shrugged and added, 'Apples.'

'Apples?' she repeated blankly.

'Mmm-hmm. Apples. I'm allergic to them.'

'You're what?' Georgina practically shrieked at him. 'Then why in the world didn't you say so?'

He shrugged again. 'To be honest, it's been so long since I ate one that I'd forgotten. I knew I didn't like apples, but I'd forgotten why, so I put it down to my mother's housewifely obsessions.' When Georgina continued to stare at him as if she wondered if he'd lost his mind, he muttered defensively, 'I didn't think about it. Besides, I ought to have outgrown the problem by now.'

'Well, you obviously haven't,' said Georgina, who was having difficulty choking back a laugh that she had a feeling would not go over well. She put a hand to her mouth then dropped it quickly.

Clayte glowered, and as she swallowed guiltily she noticed that the rash was spreading to his neck. Hastily she pulled herself together.

'What's the antidote?' she asked practically.

'I don't remember. Something the doctor gave me.'

'Antihistamines probably.' Georgina picked up the phone.

Twenty minutes later, after a brief chat with her doctor, Georgina, with a grim-faced Clayte beside her, pulled her car up in front of the Snowlake pharmacy. Hours after that, in the small hours of the morning when the two of them lay in each other's arms in her narrow bed, she put a hand to his face and said with a chuckle she no longer felt the need to suppress, 'Round one to you. I promise never again to bake you an apple pie.'

'You'd better not,' said Clayte. 'I told you I always get my way.'

'And do you always go to such drastic lengths to achieve it?' she asked pertly.

'If necessary. But I have another technique which I usually find much more effective.' He clinched his arm round her waist and leaned over to lay a trail of teasing kisses along her jawline. When he found her mouth, Georgina was obliged to admit he was right.

His kisses were much more effective.

In November, on an unusually warm and sunny afternoon, Clayton O'Neill and Georgina Kettrick were married in a quiet ceremony held in an unpretentious stone chapel beside the lake.

Georgina's parents came from Florida, looking more prosperous than she'd expected, and playing to the hilt the roles of mother and father of the bride. She had enormous difficulty keeping a straight face when her normally flamboyant and over-made-up mother stepped off the plane dressed discreetly in sober grey and white.

As for her father in a pin-stripe, she had to rub her eyes—twice—before she could believe her own eyes. None the less, she was deeply touched that they had made such a concession on her behalf.

Aunt Josephine provided the antidote. Resplendent in purple and gold, she strode to her pew on Harvey's arm like an Amazon queen accepting tribute from her grateful subjects.

'About time too,' she announced in an audible mutter, as she took her place firmly in the front. 'That nephew of mine has finally come to his senses.'

Clayte, waiting patiently at the altar for his bride, turned to his aunt with a grin and remarked that just this once he agreed with her.

After that the ceremony proceeded without incident as Georgina, attended by an impressive matron-of-honour in the person of Agnes, moved serenely down the aisle to the man she loved.

Later, at a reception attended by most of the staff from the Inn, Alexander produced a wedding banquet fit for a prince and princess. His stunned kitchen workers informed Georgina with awe in their voices that he hadn't remembered to shout at them all day.

That evening, tired but deeply content, Clayte and Georgina returned to the cottage to spend the first night of the rest of their lives together in the place where they had learned how to love.

As they walked hand in hand up the path to the welcoming white door, there was a soft whirring of wings above the trees, and a cloud of pigeons, silver against the sapphire-blue sky, rose into the air and fluttered delicately over their heads.

'They're wishing us luck,' said Georgina.

'Too late.' Clayte shook his head emphatically. 'I already have all the luck I can handle, Mrs O'Neill.'

'Handle?' she exclaimed. 'If you mean me——'

'I do.' Proving his point, Clayte scooped her into his arms and bore her in laughing triumph across the threshold.

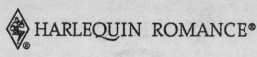 **HARLEQUIN ROMANCE®**

brings you

More Romances Celebrating Love, Families and Children!

Harlequin Romance #3362

THE BABY BUSINESS

by

Rebecca Winters

If you love babies—this book is for you!

When hotel nanny Rachel Ellis searches for her lost brother, she meets his boss—the dashing and gorgeous Vincente de Raino. She is unprepared for her strong attraction to him, but even more unprepared to be left holding the baby—his adorable baby niece, Luisa, who makes her long for a baby of her own!

Available in May wherever Harlequin Books are sold.

HARLEQUIN®

PRESENTS
RELUCTANT BRIDEGROOMS

Two beautiful brides, two unforgettable romances...
two men running for their lives....

My Lady Love, by Paula Marshall, introduces
Charles, Viscount Halstead, who lost his memory
and found himself employed as a stableboy by the
untouchable Nell Tallboys, Countess Malplaquet.
But Nell didn't consider Charles untouchable—
not at all!

Darling Amazon, by Sylvia Andrew, is the story of
a spurious engagement between Julia Marchant
and Hugo, marquess of Rostherne—an engagement
that gets out of hand and just may lead Hugo to
the altar after all!

Enjoy two madcap Regency weddings this May,
wherever Harlequin books are sold.

REG5

HARLEQUIN ROMANCE®

brings you

Harlequin Romance #3361, *Mail-Order Bridegroom*,
in our Sealed with a Kiss series next month is by one of
our most popular authors, Day Leclaire.

Leah Hampton needs a husband for her ranch
to survive—a strictly no-nonsense business arrangement.
Advertising for one in the local newspaper makes good
sense, but she finds to her horror a reply from none other
than Hunter Pryde, the man she had been in love with
eight years before!

Is her fate sealed with one kiss? Or can she resist falling
in love with him all over again?

In the coming months, look for these exciting
Sealed with a Kiss stories:

Harlequin Romance #3366
P.S. I Love You by Valerie Parv in June

Harlequin Romance #3369
Wanted: Wife and Mother by Barbara McMahon in July

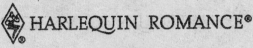

⬥ HARLEQUIN ROMANCE®

celebrates

FAMILY TIES!

**Join us in June for our brand-new miniseries—
Family Ties!**

Family… What does it bring to mind? The trials and
pleasures of children and grandchildren, loving parents
and close bonds with brothers and sisters—that special
joy a close family can bring. Whatever meaning it has for
you, we know you'll enjoy these heartwarming love stories
in which we celebrate family—and in which you can
meet some fascinating members of our
heroes' and heroines' families.

The first title to look out for is…
Simply the Best
by Catherine Spencer

followed by…

Make Believe Marriage
by Renee Roszel in July

FT-G-R

Harlequin invites you to the most
romantic wedding of the season.

Rope the cowboy of your dreams in
Marry Me, Cowboy!

A collection of 4 brand-new stories,
celebrating weddings, written by:

New York Times bestselling author

JANET DAILEY

and favorite authors

Margaret Way
Anne McAllister
Susan Fox

Be sure not to miss Marry Me, Cowboy!
coming this April

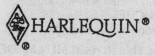

MMC

Fifty red-blooded, white-hot, true-blue hunks
from every State in the Union!

Look for MEN MADE IN AMERICA! Written by some
of our most popular authors, these stories feature some
of the strongest, sexiest men, each from a different state
in the union!

Two titles available every month at your favorite
retail outlet.

In April, look for:

FOR THE LOVE OF MIKE
by Candace Schuler (Texas)
THE DEVLIN DARE
by Cathy Thacker (Virginia)

In May, look for:

A TIME AND A SEASON
by Curtiss Ann Matlock (Oklahoma)
SPECIAL TOUCHES
by Sharon Brondos (Wyoming)

You won't be able to resist MEN MADE IN AMERICA!